HIDDEN
— NISTAR —

BATYA CASPER

AuthorReputationPress®
Creativity & Branding

Author Reputation Press LLC
45 Dan Road Suite 5
Canton MA 02021
www.authorreputationpress.com
Hotline: 1(800) 220-7660
Fax: 1(855) 752-6001

Ordering Information:
Quantity sales. Special discounts are available on quantity purchases by corporations, associations, and others. For details, contact the publisher at the address above.

Printed in the United States of America.

ISBN-13:   Softcover   978-1-64961-172-7
                 eBook   978-1-64961-173-4

Library of Congress Control Number: 2020922130

Contents

Everything is different here. No contradictions, no fiddling with ideologies, moral codes, religions, regulations—all of which depleted me so when I was mortal.

I couldn't bear the burden.

So I'll tell you what happened. I'll tell it my way, the way I understand things now, with that unearthly new knack I have of seeing myself from a distance, of getting into other people's heads.

And because, contrary to much-touted opinion, the door was wide open when I arrived here, with not a soul to weigh me in—I'll ask you to be my judge.

———oo◦◖◗◦oo———

On October 30, 1968, Baruch Lazamof, my widower, love of my youth, stumbled with a clatter and a moan out of one of the upper rooms and down the stairs. Our house had two small bedrooms and a bathroom over those stairs, and a larger room downstairs, next to the whitewashed kitchen. It was a sparsely furnished house, its cleanliness serving only to echo the silence.

Rosa, the housekeeper who found Mr. L, told the ambulance team that he'd lost his appetite in the last year or so, had become thin—bony even, the haunted expression on his face emphasized by the brown marks and the stubble that dotted his cheeks. The neighbors said it was Hannah who'd killed him, Hannah whom no one had seen in years.

Rosa told the paramedics that in the three years she'd been coming to clean, she'd never set eyes on Hannah. "Last year, on each of the six days it took our soldiers to fight the war," she said, "Mr. L left his granddaughter and me in the shelter to the sirens and the missiles flying any which way around us. He left us there while he climbed back upstairs to knock on Hannah's door and beg her to come down where it was safe. You'd think she'd have pity on him, no matter what her problem."

Rosa said she wouldn't have known Hannah's name at all if it hadn't been so clearly written in the letter three years back with its Jerusalem postmark and her—Rosa's—first Lazamof check. "Hannah," the letter had said, "she lives in the upstairs room and she likes her privacy." During her entire time of coming and going, the housekeeper had never heard so much as a sigh or a moan from the second upstairs room, though occasionally, when Baruch was fiddling with his stuff in the back shed, she thought she heard footsteps overhead.

Whether she heard them or not, the letter clearly stipulated that the mistress of that room liked to be left alone; that she must sleep, eat, and pee up there without disturbance; that she, Rosa, should never mention Hannah to Mr. Lazamof—and that's the way they liked it.

"The very first letter I received," Rosa, still trying to explain the situation, "told me it was my job to cook for Baruch Lazamof, send the little girl to school, and clean everything but that second upstairs room."

Every envelope that arrived after that with subsequent checks from the Lazamofs said the same thing. Don't clean the second bedroom. Don't go in there. Don't even open the door. Leave her a plate of toast and salad with a slab of feta cheese on top outside her room each morning (never forget the feta cheese); rice, eggs, and olives in the afternoon (don't forget the olives) before you leave.

The head paramedic—Mike, his name was—believed Baruch Lazamof had fallen down the stairs the evening before he was found. He said he could tell by the state of the bruises, the stiffness, and the temperature of Mr. Lazamof's skin.

Clearly, Rosa was upset. "He was perfectly fine the day before I found him," she kept mumbling, as though it would have been better if he'd suffered first.

It was in the morning that Rosa found him, folded over the bottom step, unconscious. Could Hannah have come out of her room and pushed Mr. L down the stairs? For sure, Rosa kept that thought to herself.

The neighbors realized it must have been the housekeeper who'd carried Baruch up to his bed. Later, they assumed it was she who'd summoned the stranger to come in on the first bus and mourn the Lazamofs, "God rest their souls." Because the day after Baruch Lazamof passed on, a woman with tinted red hair and way too much eye makeup appeared on the Lazamofs' doorstep.

She was carrying what looked to the neighbors like an old-fashioned carpetbag, the kind you used to see in spy movies, and was wearing a purple jacket over a yellow dress and boots. She seemed no more than thirty-three, thirty-four tops, walked up to what was now Hannah's front door and let herself in with a key, as though she lived there, visited occasionally, or even owned a key that belonged to that lock.

But no, Rosa told the neighbors that when she'd arrived that morning, she'd found a woman, curly-haired and thin, sitting at the kitchen table, drawing ghoulish faces on a notepad. The woman had an unnatural pallor to her cheeks and a mug of arrack and warm milk (the arrack well aged and taken from Baruch's dresser) in her left hand.

"Good morning, I'm Rosa," and she'd waited for a reply. The stranger drowned out the ghouls in red ink and sat there, didn't even lift her head to answer, so Rosa, who really was a fine human being, hung her poncho on the laundry room hook, took her apron from the kitchen drawer and the broom from its closet.

"Who are you?"

"The housekeeper," though Rosa felt she should be the one asking questions.

"Well then," and the woman stopped talking as though that was all she had to say. Rosa went back to her sweeping.

Three minutes passed, four. Finally the woman looked at Rosa, "I'm the next of kin."

Rosa pushed the second chair under the table. The woman chewed on her pen. "No need to panic. I'm not about to steal the candlesticks."

"You want tea? Coffee?"

"I have what I need, thanks," and the stranger went back to her spiral notebook and Baruch's milk-spoiled arrack.

She hadn't even inquired about the deceased. Yet after Rosa opened the blinds and sloshed soapy water over the tiles, when she was standing with her back to dead Mr. Lazamof's next of kin preparing Hannah's breakfast tray, the woman began to chat.

"Food looks good. Is it for Hannah?"

"Yes."

"How do you do that?"

"Do what?"

"How do you give it to her? The food, that is."

"I leave it outside her room, as instructed."

"Been working here long, have you?"

"Since Mrs. Lazamof died, may her memory be for a blessing."

"You've never opened her door?"

"I never even tried until less than a week ago, after Mr. Lazamof fell down the stairs. I tried to open it then, but it was locked."

"How do you give it to her now that he's dead?"

"Same as always. As I said, I leave it outside her room, on the floor."

"Which room?"

"The one on the left."

The next of kin draped her jacket over her chair, took the tray of salad and feta cheese from Rosa's hands, and carried it upstairs. Rosa heard her place the tray on the floor outside Hannah's bedroom. She heard her knock on the door. Knock a little louder. Louder still.

"Hannah," the woman was trying to turn the knob, her voice thick as gravel, "open up." Nothing. No response.

Rosa tiptoed to the foot of the stairs, her dishtowel still in her hands. "Hannah," the stranger whispering now, leaning on the door. "It's me, Sarah."

Okay then, Rosa thought, the next of kin has a name.

Like a child, Sarah slid into a kneeling position against the door. "Enough already, Hannah," whimpering now, alternately whimpering and wheezing, "There's no one left. It's three years since Pnina died. Now Baruch has gone too."

And Sarah crumpled into a yellow lump at the foot of the closed door; rocked herself silently back and forth, back and forth, as though she had a stomachache or were comforting a baby, gnawing on her thumb.

—∘∘[◦]∘∘—

Hannah

For as long as she could remember, Hannah saw herself in her pale wooden frame directly in her parents' line of vision, smiling like a puppy with her head on her hands, telling the self that was watching her, "I'm happy here, you see, like this. I don't want to change." But when the child with the transparent hair grew outside of that frame as she was forced to do and developed into her redheaded reality, change was already happening.

As for Jacob, he grew taller and sweeter with each passing day, Hannah thought. In the picture that had stood forever on the now-warped bureau, Jacob had no need to change. His impish grin, at the same time shy and challenging, never faded. Sharing a joke with the photographer perhaps, the sun shining on him too. And on Simeon, on Simeon's slanted smile and hypnotic eyes, though in that snapshot she never could get herself to look into Simeon's eyes.

The framed version of Jacob was the way Hannah wanted to remember him always: an acorn face with a cap that was too big for him because it was his father's. The cap was riding on an army of curls, hair that bubbled up from his otherwise acorn head until he was at least eight years old. Affectionate. Plopped down on that spot in the picture after a run up their hill, the one in front of their house, beyond the scope of the camera.

Tikvah

1963

T ikvah lived with us, Pnina and Baruch Lazamof, at the top of the hill, in the first and oldest house of our village. When Tikvah was small, I did what she supposed other grandmothers did when they got home from work: shopped, cleaned, helped my grandchild, albeit grudgingly, with homework, and went into the village once in a while—please, please—to buy something, anything at all. I only talked when necessary. By that stage of my life, sighing was my communication of choice, and, God knows, I did a great deal of that.

For the most part, my bulbous body reclined in my armchair opposite what Mr. L called the Lazamof art gallery: three photographs that constituted the collection of our home. In those days, only one subject was capable of raising me to a state of interest, of conversation even: it was those pictures.

The image on the left was of two boys whom I called Jacob and Simeon.

"Where are they now?"

"They grew up years ago, Tikvah. Left the country when you were still tiny, before you could even crawl."

"Yes, but who are they?"

"Boys. Boys who lived in our village. Stop with your questions. I'm tired." And I heaved my body over to face the wall.

Tikvah knew the picture well: The missing front tooth in Jacob's smile, curls under an oversized cap; the way Simeon's mouth smiled farther up the right side of his face than the left, his freckles, his eyes that she knew were talking to her though she couldn't hear their words.

The picture in the middle, browner in tone than the first with random dark spots over the background, which Tikvah called "old people's skin," showed a muscular man in an open shirt and straw hat sitting on a horse. I rolled back from the wall.

"He was a Cossack."

"What's a Cossack?"

"A man who can ride a horse."

That was the one funny thing I ever said. It made Baruch chuckle. But Tikvah wouldn't give up. "Who was he?"

"I told you. A man on a horse."

"Why is it funny a man on a horse?"

"Funny?" I really was a pain in those days. "It's not funny to me."

"Oh. Why is he hanging on our wall?"

"Where'd you want him to hang?"

I snorted and rolled over again, again signifying an end to Tikvah's questions.

Like the people in the other pictures, that man had looked out at us from what my husband called "our Lazamof wall" for as long as Tikvah could remember, his right hand permanently shading his eyes from the sun, forever mounted on his horse. Tikvah never ceased to admire that horse; its size, its power, its giant feet firmly planted on a hillside similar to our own, she thought, but that spread down, way down to the sea, without a house in sight.

Toward the right of the wall hung "a woman in her middle years." That phrase and "buxom" was the way Mr. L's younger son, Michael, described her on every one of his yearly visits. The woman stood ramrod straight on the flat part of her field draped in a voluminous skirt and white blouse, her hair transparent in the sunlight, long, but pinned to the back of her head. A cameo with an image on it too small for Tikvah to see hung from the woman's throat.

Under one arm, she was holding what looked like a tub, the iron kind people once used for washing clothes. Her other arm was held out, palm facing upward, her face also turned toward the sky, smiling—even laughing perhaps—at the birds. Because the air around the woman's head was filled with seagulls, winged creatures swirling around her as though she were their mother and they her children, Tikvah thought, children of the air.

She has the happy face and the bearing ("bearing," Mr. L's word) of a fun woman, Tikvah whispered to herself, an energetic, joyful woman, nothing like Mrs. L. But then Tikvah felt mean. Who knows, she thought, how that woman felt when she wasn't smiling for her picture.

"Why won't you tell me who they were?"

"People, Tikvah, they were people."

"What kind of people? Did we know them?"

"How would I know what kind? People who died a long time ago." Tikvah crossed to the far corner of the room, curled herself into a ball.

"Why don't you have pictures of my parents?"

"They didn't leave any."

"What were their names?"

"I've already told you: Aba and Ima."

"Dad and Mom aren't names."

"Knowing their names won't bring them back, Tikvah. Don't bother me anymore. I'm tired."

Tears welled in Tikvah's eyes. "Why won't you tell me anything? Why won't you talk to me?"

But this, for me, had been a lengthy conversation. My voice was dry, Tikvah told herself, because I rarely breathed air. Other reasons, Tikvah thought, might have been that I'd suffered from what Michael called existential exhaustion for years, and that I never moved when I didn't absolutely have to.

Now that Tikvah was six and a half, and I'd trained her to keep her bed made, her body clean, and her curls away from her face in dark braids down her back, I could come home each day from my work at the bank and "get horizontal," as I liked to call it. Once that happened, I rarely got up again. Not to eat. Not to wash the dishes. Not to clean the floor or swipe ants from the counter. I left those to my long-suffering husband, and to Tikvah.

The way Tikvah saw it, I knitted when I was awake, wheezed when I talked, mumbled in my sleep, and invariably woke with a start and a scream as though a car, or a building, or, God forbid, a person had been blown to smithereens.

I was allergic to fresh air. Consequently, days went by without anyone opening the windows, and our little blue-eyed Tikvah learned not to breathe when she came home from school until she got used to the smell. Our names were Baruch and Pnina; we were her *saba* and *savta*, which means grandpa and grandma, but Tikvah decided early on to call us by our formal titles: Mr. and Mrs. Lazamof, so that, for the most part, is how I will refer to us from now on—in the third person.

Mr. L had sturdy limbs, sun-wrinkled skin, and piercing green eyes. He reminded Tikvah of the picture on top of the English Sharp Toffees box, the one with the top hat and the cane, with the striped pants and black jacket, that was kept on the import shelf at the grocery store, covered in dust.

Not that Mr. L was nearly that well dressed, or looked even vaguely like that picture; but he had style, "a style of his own," as his son, Michael, liked to tell Tikvah. He wore a vest, "brocade," is what he said it was, of several shades of brown blended snugly on his chest, satin at the back, nibbled by moths and frayed at the edges. He had a silver pocket watch threaded through his buttonhole and hidden in his vest pocket where it ticked like a dislodged heart on all except summer days.

The only things he wore in summer were undershirts and shorts held up by a broad leather belt. A handkerchief peeked permanently from his back pants pocket. "That?" he told Tikvah, "that's my flag of surrender."

But the dapper features of Mr. Lazamof, the features Tikvah loved most about his appearance, were the red scarf that he tucked into the V of his cardigan on winter months and the leather hat he'd bought years back at the souk, the outdoor market, which he wore flat on his head, like cow turd. He wore shoes overlaid with white leather at the toes, which shone with a yellowish gleam like antique mirrors.

Mr. Lazamof's watch, he told Tikvah, had come over with him from Russia. His shoes he'd bought at the end of the Mandate from a British officer with marching orders. "I danced to the birth of Israel in them," he told her, "our great hurrah of independence before our neighbors attacked." Mr. L paused to wipe sweat from his brow. "Beat the crap out of us, they did, and we did the same for them."

For most of his adult life, Mr. L kept his treasures in the bottom draw of his dresser, until one day when he took them out and said, "If not now, when?"

"In Russia," he told Tikvah, "clothes signified something," though he never told her what. The village they lived in was only four streets square. All we need do, Tikvah thought, is walk half a mile, and we'll reach the twentieth century where fashion is available and tempting in any store.

But that hadn't happened since she'd been around. And she'd been around for as long as she could remember. It was clear to her that Mr. Lazamof's Israel had failed him in the style department.

"Your grandfather is a champion chess player," Michael told her on one of his annual visits. Michael was Mr. L's younger son from a previous marriage. "He's famous. People challenge him from all over town." Tikvah hadn't seen "people"; barely a person, in fact. Besides, it was a village they lived in, not a town, but she liked Michael, so she believed him.

"Come," Mr. Lazamof told her one day when Mrs. L was napping in her chair, moaning in her sleep, "I'll teach you to play." Five minutes or less into the game, he turned the pallid smile Tikvah loved so much toward her. "Congratulations, you've won."

Tikvah didn't ask how that could have happened in so short a time. "Wake up, Mrs. L. I beat Mr. Lazamof! I beat him at chess! I'm a champion, Mrs. Lazamof, wake up!"

But nothing was going to wake Pnina Lazamof once she'd escaped into her nap.

No one was there to hear Tikvah in her triumphant hour, so she ran down the street to the Hakims. But Annyush Hakim had three grandchildren staying with them while her son and daughter-in-law were at work. They were so busy they didn't even see her standing there. When she forced the youngest Hakim to squat on the stone floor opposite her, take his pacifier out of his mouth, and listen, he didn't understand what she was saying.

No one cared.

It was like the story Mr. Lazamof had told her, which she never did understand, of the tree that falls in the forest without making a noise. The thing is—and she knew it was strange, way too strange to tell anyone—so many times she sensed in the deepest part of herself that she, Tikvah, was that self same tree. Sometimes—that precise moment was an example—she felt herself falling, and though she was absolutely certain a scream was reverberating throughout her body and brain loud enough for the angels above (which she hoped existed) to hear her, she couldn't. Couldn't hear the sound. Couldn't hear the noise she was making. No one could.

Did that mean she wasn't screaming, she wanted to know—that she hadn't fallen, that she hadn't won the chess game, or that maybe she wasn't there at all?

Because so often she felt that the Lazamof life wasn't the one she was destined to lead, that she wouldn't begin her own existence until she was somewhere else entirely. Perhaps she should run away to someone who'd tell her who her parents were, perhaps to Michael and Noam?—though they'd always changed the subject when she'd asked. Still, she knew they'd take her in despite their not being full blood relatives.

Then she thought of Mr. L—his freckled forehead. In her mind's eye, she saw his funny, crooked smile. He'd looked her seriously in the face when she'd asked, and said, "I can't tell you now, sweetness, but I promise to when you grow up." He was her grandfather, her *Saba*. No. She'd never run away from him.

Tikvah stood still on her way back from the Hakims' house, smelling the pines, talking to the cones, to the needles that crunched underfoot. Out loud, she said, "If this is not my life, what is?"

But the pines and their fallen cones had their own existence to endure.

They didn't even know she was there.

Mrs. L told Tikvah that Noam and Michael, Mr. Lazamof's bachelor sons, were not to be confused with full-blood relatives. Tikvah didn't know what "blood relatives" were, either full or partial, though she was sure grateful hers were not.

Regardless of blood, Noam and Michael visited each year on the High Holidays. Each year, Noam brought Tikvah licorice, the large red rope kind, her favorite, and a new dress; and Michael, new shoes, always the same, shiny black with delicate straps and tiny silver buckles, and pale blue ribbons for her hair so beautiful they made her feel like fiction—like an unreal girl in a story book.

Noam was tall like his birth mother. He spoke with a lisp. He wore khaki shirts with sleeves folded at least four centimeters above his elbows, and sandals that curled up at the front over his toes. Michael was short and slight; he took after his father. His skin was darker than Noam's, and he had a mustache that reminded Tikvah of summer grass.

"Why aren't you married?" she asked every year, though she knew Noam's wife had left him, and every year both brothers responded with the same answer: "Because we've not found anyone as pretty as you." Every year she giggled and ran away so they wouldn't see how pleased she was.

New Year's morning, Mr. Lazamof and his sons dressed in starched white shirts. Noam wore blue cotton pants each year, and Michel khaki ones, both with a ruler-straight crease down the center.

Tikvah pirouetted in front of the hall mirror in her wide-skirted dress and shiny shoes.

"What color thould I bring you necth year?" That's what Noam's lisp sounded like.

"White, it's my favorite color."

"Silly," Michael said, every year, "white's not a color."

"It's what I like the most."

So the dress Noam brought her was always white, and though always too long, never failed to transform her into a princess, and their otherwise brown and dingy home into a place of beauty and light.

As for Mrs. L, she claimed that gifts were for people with dreams in their heads," as though that were a bad thing, so they never brought her any. Mrs. L's gray dress, with its miniscule strip of velvet across the neckline, hung bosom-less in the closet throughout the year waiting for the holiday season, and that is what she wore. No frills.

Instead, Noam and Michael brought her cake, which she set next to her home-baked pastries on the table over her once-a-year lace cloth. They brought Mr. L arrack to add to his collection. Glass bowls—three amber, three red—of dates, figs, and pomegranate seeds stood near his silver holiday cups waiting for "his ladies" to come home from prayers. Mr. L never went with them. Neither did his sons.

"Come with us to the service, please, just this once."

"We're agnostics."

"We don't serve."

"They won't want uth there anyway," Noam added.

"Why not?"

"Becauth we don't believe."

"What don't you believe in?"

"You name it, thweetness, we don't believe in it—that'th what 'agnothtic' meanth."

"Right," Mrs. L rolled her eyes. "And you wonder why your wife walked out on you."

"Mrs. L, am I an agnostic?"

"Now, why would you be such a thing?"

"Because my parents walked out on me too."

"Don't talk nonsense, Tikvah. You are not agnostic. Loads of children live without their parents. It's unfortunate, but that's the way it is. Come. Help me with the food."

As much as Tikvah wanted to be like the men in her family, she was relieved she wasn't agnostic. For her, even the fast day that followed the New Year was cause for celebration, because, as Mr. L said, "the Days of Awe are the season of Mrs. Lazamof's content, the clarion call to her awakening." Like a bear emerging from hibernation, Mrs. L rose from her armchair exactly ten days prior to the New Year, donned her apron, cleaned, cooked, and visited dead people at the cemetery.

Nineteen sixty-five was the year Mrs. L resigned from normal living, the year Tikvah turned nine. That was a year of uncertainty, for sure. Neither Mr. L nor Tikvah knew what to expect as the holiday season came around. Yet, lo and behold, ten days before the holidays, Tikvah's grandmother stood up. Mr. L called it "Mrs. Lazamof's rising."

Rising or not, Mrs. L refused to take Tikvah with her to the cemetery. "You don't have any business there. You don't know those people."

Tikvah was determined. She sneaked several steps behind her grandmother on her journey through the village, prepared to dash behind trees or inside doorways if she turned around. She didn't. Who would have believed? Mrs. L, who for a year had not pried herself from her chair for anything but bank or bathroom, was charging to the cemetery with focus, vigor, and determination. Once there, she disappeared among the graves.

Forty-five minutes later, she emerged. Tikvah was waiting by the gateway, bracing herself for confrontation.

"Are my parents buried in there?"

And for the first and only time, her grandmother told her.

"No, dear." Mrs. L never called her "dear."

"Your parents are buried in the desert."

They began their walk home.

"What were they doing in the desert?"

"Protecting our country from harm."

"Both of them?"

"Yes."

"Did they die together?"

"Yes. They wanted to because they loved each other a lot."

"What did they die of?"

"Your father died of bravery, your mother of gentleness."

"Gentleness?"

"Yes, gentle people get called from this world earlier than others."

"Mr. L is gentle."

"And brave too, though not overly so. He's the right amount of gentle and brave for this world."

Mrs. L. She's enough to make you scream.

———◦◦◦❖◦◦◦———

The Sons of Jacob was built in the 1930s by parents and grandparents of its current members, long before Israel was declared a state. It was the oldest public structure in their village: an unassuming, two-story building with crumbling stucco walls whitewashed each year in honor of the holidays.

Though the Lazamofs and their neighbors were more than half done with the twentieth century, and universities and technical schools were in full force just fifty kilometers away, chickens from neighboring homes still waddled over during prayers to cluck and peck in the synagogue yard. Grand-chickens, Tikvah told herself, of their slaughtered founding fathers.

The Sons of Jacob had stained-glass windows under a tile roof that was low and did nothing to mitigate the heat. In the early pre-state days, the space beneath that roof was used to stash guns and take up arms against marauding Arabs. Today, there were no marauding Arabs, just snipers along the border and shots in the night. Women clomped up the stairs in their freshly polished shoes merely to pray in their assigned section. On the top step, they caught their breath, nodded to each other, selected their prayer books from the shelf and peered over the men below.

It was early. There was still time before the sun grew hot. The rabbi's wife, always the first to arrive, threw the windows open so the synagogue was washed with tree-scented air and morning breezes— without the slightest objection from the newly risen Mrs. Lazamof. Light hovered over the congregants in colored streamers through the stained glass and across the room where it celebrated on the newly painted walls. Tikvah gasped. It's Mrs. L's miracle, she thought; the season of her awakening.

The air was cool when the celebrants began the service, humming in a gentle cadence, soft and low, thanking the creator of all things for bounties given. It was cool when all the villagers finally arrived and the Sons of Jacob reverberated with song. It was not yet hot when the men took the Torah scrolls from the ark and chanted the holiday portion, bodies swaying— women on their upstairs balcony, men in the hall below. But when the sun reached the tiled roof of the Sons of Jacob, the hall heated up and the chanting sighed like a chiffon scarf sinking to the ground.

It was then that a hush fell over the Sons of Jacob, each adult shrinking farther from her neighbors, deeper into herself, mouthing words no one else could hear. Urgency had taken hold, silent but present. Tikvah felt it. Promises were being made in secret that Tikvah couldn't understand. Bargains contracted between each woman, on their previously cozy balcony, and her maker, between other women's husbands, other girls' grandfathers swaying in the hall below, and their God.

Tikvah watched it happen—men blowing their noses, women allowing tears to fall unchecked over their books of prayer.

Grown women and adult men were sobbing now, in the secrecy of their hearts, over the lives they'd led, mistakes they'd made, loved ones they'd hurt or were neglecting, and those who'd been stolen from them.

Tikvah squirmed then slumped low in her seat, her head down, wiggling her toes. Good times never lasted—not in this village, and for sure never by Mrs. L's side.

By Mrs. L's side good times came only in spurts separated by endless dead spaces, the way Mr. L had described Morse code to her. Why did she always forget that? Why was she always taken in by the first hint of action?

Yet, of all possible moments, Mrs. L chose that one, in which Tikvah was thinking those particularly hostile thoughts, to lean in and hold Tikvah's hand. Mrs. L never held her hand. "You're a good girl, Tikvale. Don't think I can't see that."

Mrs. L had never said anything like that before. She'd never called her "Tikvale" before. Tikvah's face flushed hot and sticky. She slunk even lower into her seat. She bit her lip till it hurt.

She was sitting between Mrs. L and the remaining women of their village, all squeezed into the front row of their balcony because Mrs. L said their village was shrinking (an image that made Tikvah's skin tingle), more villagers leaving for the cities with each passing year. Light hovered over them in shafts of shifting colors as the men paraded the Torah scrolls round the synagogue, the crowns and the tiny silver bells tinkling as they passed, Tikvah—even Mrs. L— blowing kisses.

Mothers drew their children down the stairs to kiss the scrolls. Tikvah pouted, "I don't wanna be here anymore, I wanna go home."

———•••◉•••———

The kids of their village had grown and moved away, so Tikvah, Annyush Hakim's grandchildren, and the youngest members of the rabbi's family were the only members left under the age of ten. Nevertheless, at the end of the holy season, tradition being tradition, Tikvah and the visiting grandchildren were huddled downstairs under the beadle's massive prayer shawl that smelled of peppermints and old wine, and the rabbi blessed them.

The rabbi's bony wife presented the kids with honey-apples on sticks, and the women, Mrs. Lazamof included, leaned from their upstairs railing and threw candies at their heads.

———•••◉•••———

"Remember Liora from high thchool?"

"What, from seventh grade, Liora Zahavi?"

"Yeah, I bumped into her on Migdal thtreet."

It was the afternoon of the holiday, after the family had gorged themselves on Mrs. L's chicken-in-olives-and-apricots, her noodle casserole, and her honey cake. Tikvah was sitting on the front steps with Mr. L's grown-up sons, cracking sunflower seeds between her teeth the way they did, listening as they talked, the pungent smell of their cigarette smoke wafting in a sophisticated trail from the Lazamofs' front step down the street to the steps of their neighbors.

"Thee'th divorthed. Left her huthband latht dethember. After fifteen yearth."

"How about that. Cute little Zahava, divorced. I always knew she was too good for that man."

"I think I'll call her. Athk her out."

"You? Call Zahava? You'd never have the nerve."

"Why would he need nerve?" Tikvah asked. "Is she scary?" But they didn't answer. They'd forgotten she was there.

Nothing more was said about Zahava on Migdal Street. Instead, Tikvah listened as Michael argued with Noam over the most profitable way of importing plants from Africa and growing them south of their contentious northern border. She listened, marveling that some women are so strange, so scary, they frighten grown men.

———∞•◦|◯|◦•∞———

Michael and Noam left when the holidays ended. Mrs. Lazamof hung her festive dress back in its closet and returned to her chair. A month later, in the deliciously crisp air of autumn, she called the bank and resigned from her position as the oldest-looking teller there.

Her breathing was deteriorating. She stopped knitting. She groaned more in her sleep, woke up more, each time with her customary start and stifled scream. Each day, it seemed, she sank deeper into her chair, until one Friday afternoon when she stopped talking altogether. Wouldn't tell them if she wanted a glass of water or food, whether she needed their help. If they didn't guess when she needed to go to the bathroom, Mr. L. was left cleaning up her mess. If they hadn't decided when she wanted to eat, she'd have starved to death.

They opened the windows, shooing their stale air out with a dishtowel, inviting the fall to waft crisp and unimpeded through their home. Tikvah and Mr. L stood by the open glass and watched the birds gather in formation for their yearly flight across the sea. Mrs. L never said a word.

Weeks passed in which the only movement Mrs. L made was as the central figure in their bathroom convoy. Then, on the last Sunday of November, the window open, Mrs. L breakfasting on yogurt and sliced cucumber, sounds of shelling reaching them in uneven barrages from the border, Mrs. L knocked her coffee glass over. A milky stain ran down her dress and into the creases of her chair, home to God knows how many other food offerings, and she stopped eating, refused to taste another morsel.

December second, Mrs. Lazamof was still refusing to swallow. "My love," Mr. L begged, "come with me to the clinic." She wouldn't budge, so he went alone to the village center, running down the middle of their unpaved road, tripping over his own feet, as Mrs. L would have said if she'd been with him. Within thirty minutes, he was ushering the doctor in through their front door.

"Her vital signs are fine," the doctor clicking his tongue as he talked, "It seems she's had enough."

When they tried to take her to the hospital, Mrs. L clutched the arms of her chair with such sudden vigor—her face white, her lips pursed in determination—they couldn't budge her.

Mrs. L turned her face toward her husband. "Noam and Michael," her lips too dry for sound, "now."

So Mr. L's sons drove up in Noam's brand new blue Ford, despite Mrs.

L's claim that they were not full blood relatives. Mrs. L clutched their arms with her hands as they bent side by side before her, her fingers gray as the claws of a bird, her eyes hard as an eagle's. "When the time comes," she hissed at them, "you will watch over Tikvah."

"Don't worry, we'll be here."

"Promise," and she wouldn't let go of them until Mr. L brought her mother's Bible down from their bedroom, and Noam and Michael swore.

They sat by her chair for three more days, Mr. L spooning water and crushed ice between his wife's lips, stroking the gray backs of her hand, whispering, "Don't leave me, my love, the love of my life," beneath his breath, until Wednesday morning when Michael and Noam drove off to buy household supplies and Mrs. L closed her eyes.

When she did that, Mr. L bent down, thrust his face directly into little Tikvah's, grasped both her hands in his, and pulled her to him. "You're a big girl now," his voice tight and hard, "Stay here, right here. Don't move. Don't budge from her side, not even for a second. You hear me? I can rely on you, right?"

Tikvah nodded yes, though she didn't want to be relied on, not then, not there. She didn't want to stay alone in that house with her grandma who couldn't eat, talk, or open her eyes. She wanted to go with her *saba*. Because an odor had seeped into their home—not the old bad smell from the good days before Mrs. L became sick; that smell had blown away the moment they'd opened the windows. This was a thick yellow stench, heavy as a rain-drenched blanket. It had permeated everything they possessed—their clothes, the rug, the furniture, the food they ate. It hung over her grandma's chair. *Why does no one talk about it? Try to get rid of it? Haven't they noticed it?* And Tikvah knew, though she'd never encountered it before: No one was mentioning it because that stench was the messenger of death.

Mr. L left to fetch the doctor. Tikvah ran after the already closing door, a sob escaping her despite her wanting to live up to Mr. L's expectations, her body caught in a sudden icy spasm as though a midwinter wind was blowing through their house.

Amazingly, the moment the door closed, a miracle happened: Mrs. L opened her eyes. She talked.

"Tikvale." Only once before had Mrs. L called her that. Her voice was raspy, it was frail, but Tikvah had no difficulty hearing it. "Go down the street to Annyush Hakim. Tell her I've nearly finished my painkillers. Tell her I need more."

"I promised Mr. L I wouldn't leave you."

"What does he think? That I'll get up and walk away?"

"It's only eleven thirty. Miss Hakim won't be home. She's at work."

"Don't argue with me, Tikvah. I don't have the strength. I must have my painkillers. Now. Go to Miss Hakim's house. If she's not home, go to her work. Find her."

"Mr. L will be back any minute. He's bringing the doctor. The doctor will give you pills."

"Silly girl, the doctor doesn't know what I need. He has no idea what's good for me. Go."

"But I promised Mr.—"

"You want me to die of pain? Go. I need my medicine. I need it now."

"But..."

"You've always been a good girl, Tikvale, but now I need you to be a grown up. Please, without those pills, I'll die."

Tikvah started to cry. "I told Mr. L he could rely on me."

"Tikvah, sweet one. I'll tell him you went only to save my life, that you didn't want to go, that I made you."

Needless to say, Miss Hakim wasn't home. "Told you," Tikvah muttered, addressing Mrs. L under her breath. *Why doesn't she ever listen? She never listens!*

Now she had no choice but to go to Miss Hakim's place of work. She paced the sidewalk outside the Hakims' house, biting her nails, waiting for the bus. A promise was a promise, and how could she break hers to—of all the people in the world—her granddad, the sweetest person she knew, who was relying on her? He'd never trust her again. He'd never believe she was saving Mrs. L's life. She should forget about her grandma's pills and go home.

How could she do that? If she didn't bring her her medicine, Mrs. L, who was her *savta* after all, would die of pain, she'd told her she would, and Mr. L, who loved his wife more than anyone in the entire world—he would for sure die of sorrow.

It took ten whole minutes of Tikvah walking back and forth along the curb, chewing her fingernails and kicking at the stones, for the bus to come. She told herself she was wasting time, that it would be quicker to walk to Miss Hakim's pharmacy, knowing that even if she ran all the way it would take her longer than the bus, and that the bus would be there any minute.

It came. Finally. She rode from the Hakim house to First Pioneers Pharmacy where Miss Hakim worked, wondering all the while how miraculous it was that Mrs. L's strength had been so suddenly restored, and that she could talk. But Miss Hakim wasn't at the pharmacy. She'd taken the morning off to escort her granddaughter's seventh grade class to the museum. An entire week had passed in the Lazamof home, and no one had even thought to send Tikvah to school.

The assistant on pharmacy duty said she wasn't authorized to issue medicines. "Go to the clinic. They'll have your grandma's pills in their chart."

Tikvah had given her word to her *saba* that she wouldn't move, even for an instant, from Mrs. L's side. Yet here she was, already six bus stops from home. She needed to get back before Mr. L did, before he discovered that she'd broken her promise and couldn't be trusted.

But she didn't do that. She took the bus to the clinic, tearing at her fingernails with her teeth, her breath escaping from her lungs along the way in heavy, gulping sobs.

A woman in a white coat and clompy shoes told her that her *saba* had been there, that he'd left only a couple of minutes earlier with the doctor and with new pills for her grandma.

"Those pills—are they the doctor's?"

"What do you mean?"

"My grandma told me the doctor's pills don't help her. She said she needs Miss Hakim's pills."

"The pills Miss Hakim gives her are the ones the doctor prescribed. They're identical. They are what your *savta* needs."

Ugh! Grownups. They're enough to make you scream! She could have stayed home, as her *saba* had wanted.

They were there before her, all of them: Mr. L and the doctor, Michael, and Noam. As she opened the door, Michael was lifting an empty vial of pills from Mrs. L's lap.

"Look, Mrs. L broke the security wrap. This was a full bottle."

Mr. L turned as Tikvah walked into the room. "Where were you? Why did you leave her?"

19

The cabinet door was open. Mr. L's arrack bottle, the one Michael and Noam had given him for the holidays, which no one had even opened, was on the floor, empty except for the thinnest, saddest, line of liquid—and Tikvah's *savta* was dead.

Her hair—gray, combative and unyielding in life—had relinquished its curls. Noam was smoothing them backward with a wet comb, creating the impression that she might be someone else entirely. Her face was white as never before, covered in oversized sun spots, *though God only knows*, Tikvah thought, *she never spent time in the sun*. Her eyes were closed, for which Tikvah was thankful. She'd hate for Mrs. L to see her now that she'd failed her in such a huge, horrendous way.

No one spoke. Ever so gently, as though her *savta* were taking a nap, Mr. L tucked a blanket around his dead wife. The slightest noise, Tikvah felt sure—and she'd wake up.

It was cold. So cold. Tikvah began to shiver. Her body shook so violently, her bones rattled. Michael picked her up. He folded her in his jacket and carried her from that place.

For the longest time after that, Tikvah was unable to talk. Not a word. She couldn't sleep, had bad dreams, woke, screaming, in the middle of the night.

Her grandmother hadn't spared as much as a parting glance, not even a nod of farewell to sweet Mr. L who loved her so much. She'd not waited, hadn't uttered a word of good-bye to her.

Tikvah decided never to grieve for her grandmother. She stayed close to her *saba*, walked by his side, followed him everywhere. The village grew to know them as Mr. L and his shadow.

———◦◦○◦○◦———

It wasn't because Tikvah was mentally slow or anything of that nature that she'd never seen what was going on in her own home; it wasn't that she hadn't cared about what was happening around her, she had.

Her neighbors knew everything, way before her *savta* died, though they'd rarely, if ever, stepped into the Lazamofs' home, and for sure they'd never gone upstairs. They knew, for example, that the Lazamofs had an adult daughter living in one of the upstairs bedrooms the entire time Tikvah lived there, yet Tikvah never knew it. "That's the storage room," her grandparents had told her the only time she'd asked. "It's locked."

For years, in the predawn of each and every day, sweet Mr. Lazamof had set omelets, boiled chickpeas, and packets of the sunflower seeds she'd always loved outside his adult daughter's bedroom, removing the soiled dishes from the night before and the pile of dirty clothes or sheets that were waiting for him. He repeated the ritual late each night.

Tikvah slept in the downstairs room. On a night in 1962 of rain and thunder, she woke, scared and whimpering, and climbed to the second floor.

"*Saba*, I had a nightmare."

"A nightmare is only a dream, sweetness. Come, we'll go back to your room, and you'll tell me about it."

"Why are there sheets out here, on the landing?"

"That's where we put them when we change the bed. I take them downstairs in the morning."

"What is that plate doing here?"

"It's food I leave out for Mrs. L. She often wakes up hungry during the night. Want some?"

Mr. L spread a blanket round Tikvah's shoulders. They perched on the top stair munching chickpeas and cracking sunflower seeds. Tikvah's nightmare floated like smoke from her mind, and she fell asleep.

——∘∘〗◉〖∘∘——

Mr. L came up with a scheme. He devoted a month to imagining it, seven nights to planning—Mrs. L next to him on the bed sighing, whimpering even, in her sleep—and three more weeks studying diagrams in the library. Then, one warm, moonless night, he got out of bed, looked through the window into the darkness, walked down to the kitchen table, and drew the first of his sketches.

In the colorless hours of the following dawn, he was pacing outside the hardware store waiting for it to open. He bought nails, hammers, metal strips, wire, and wood. Within four months, he'd constructed a staircase that reached from the grassless patch at the back of their house to Hannah's upstairs window.

Mr. L returned to the store. He bought a toy trumpet, loud enough to empty hell of its devils, and a flashlight. At exactly midnight, he stood in the darkness at the back of his house, blew three long blasts on his trumpet, and shone his flashlight through his daughter's window.

Little Tikvah was trembling, whimpering in the doorway as he crept back into the house. "What was that noise?"

"Go back to sleep, sweetness. It was just the military testing its sirens." He carried her to her room, tucked her back into bed, and held her hand until her eyes closed and her breathing steadied. Then he went back to his own room.

"You'll see, Pnina. This is going to work. It will bring Hannah back."

"Fool," Mrs. L answered in the darkness. "She's no longer of this world."

The next morning, Mr. L slipped the key to his daughter's window under her door.

Mr. L couldn't listen to his wife. He walked to the library, borrowed books, and left them outside Hannah's room. For six weeks, romances, historical novels, and poetry lay rejected where they'd been placed, causing little Tikvah to ask why there were books on the landing and whether they were meant for the storage room. The plates of food disappeared and appeared again in the dead of night, empty of food. But books were rejected.

Mr. L consulted the librarian.

"Ora, what would you recommend for a woman who won't read?"

"Picture magazines," and Ora directed him to the periodical room.

Mr. L brought food journals, journals about American movie stars, about travel, about how to apply makeup, and how to improve your love life. All were rejected. *What does she want from me?* Mr. L thought. *I didn't write that stuff.*

Friday evening, just before the library closed, he found a stack of out-of-date, much-used magazines on the bottom of the used pamphlet rack entitled, *Everything You Want to Know About Wild Birds.*

Like magic, the bird journals were sucked in from the landing. Three days later, there they were, all five of them outside Hannah's room, pages folded at the corners, covers smudged more than before. "Thank you God, my bountiful God," whispered Mr. L the agnostic. "We have a plan."

Each week, he scoured the library for bird journals, until one rainy afternoon before the Hanukah holiday when Ora suggested he subscribe to the Literary Society of Birds and Butterflies. "They deliver two editions per week, directly to your home."

Mr. L kissed Ora smack on the mouth, hugged her until she could no longer breathe, danced her round the periodical room with her gasping and giggling until the school kid who was trying to do his homework ran for cover, and wept like a baby.

Nothing could stop Mr. L now. He ran through the rain, in and out of the stores, all about to close. He bought a transistor radio, a big, black, cumbersome one with oversized knobs. He bought the evening newspaper, four raspberry doughnuts—it was a day before the Hanukah holiday and the store was down to its final four—and a tiny silver pendant that was suspended by its chain over the counter, shaped like the jagged half of a heart.

Mr. L set his offerings where he'd set all the others. By morning, they were gone. That night, the radio and the newspaper were ejected. Mr. L was content.

For the first night in so many, he felt almost calm as he climbed into bed, calm enough to confront his wife. "Pnina, my love," his hand placed gently on her back, "Tikvah is growing. She's asking questions."

Silence. Mrs. Lazamof didn't move.

"We'll have to answer them."

Mrs. L turned. "No! Don't dare! Do you want another broken spirit in this house? Don't we have enough?" She clambered out of bed, paced around the room, shuffled beneath the chair for her slippers, gave that up, and leaned over her husband. "Tikvah is whole. She's okay. She has a chance at the good life. Would you rob her of that?" She plodded over to her bureau and brought her Bible, the one she'd brought so many years earlier from her parents' home. "Swear. Swear on the Bible that you will never tell her. That you'll let her grow to be normal."

That night, after his wife had fallen asleep, Mr. L slipped out of their house. He walked the two blocks to Ora, the librarian's house. Didn't come home till dawn.

———◦◦◦❧◦◦◦———

Not long after that, a woman appeared in the village, sitting on a park bench late at night. A couple of nights later, she appeared at the bus stop, mumbling to herself in her beige raincoat, the paper-thin kind you can fold up and keep in your pocket, her hair matted and long, shielding her face from view. Two weeks after that, the village doctor saw the woman as he was driving home from the hospital. She was walking away from the cinema as the late show was emptying out, cradling an injured bird in her arm.

One evening toward the end of January, the woman stepped from a winter storm into the library wearing men's pants under her raincoat. Her coat was open, her pants were soaking wet, and a lake of rain was dripping off her onto the floor. Ora brought her her own heart-shaped mug of coffee. The woman ignored it. Instead, she wandered around the bookshelves until she found the wildlife section, dripping rain.

Ora snuck into the back room and called Mr. L. "There's a woman here. Can you believe it, in this weather? She's reading bird magazines." It took less than ten minutes for Mr. L to reach the library, but the woman was no longer there. Neither was the librarian's heart-shaped mug. Ora had bent down to pick up a coin from the floor. When she stood up, the woman was gone.

Mr. L pounded the rain-drenched streets until way after midnight looking for the woman. He never found her.

It was one of those magical afternoons in February that look and feel like summer. Mr. Caspi opened the door of his pharmacy for just a moment between customers to feel the sun against his body; there was the woman on his sidewalk, VITA MAGIC looming over her head. Her eyes were closed, her men's pants pushed up above her knees, and her shirt buttons open. The sun was shining directly on her freckled face, and an orange alley cat, one of a gang that scavenged under the tables of the coffee shop, was nestled over her raincoat in her lap.

On the first day of spring, after a really dry winter, the school principal was walking to work when she saw the woman squatting on the grass near the road, lighting a circle of shrubs with a match. As the principal watched, the flames leapt into a fire threatening the trees and nearby buildings. She called the fire station. Three giant trucks roared up the street, bells and lights flashing, sirens blasting. A crowd formed. The woman disappeared. The firemen put the fire out, doused the field with their hoses, and asked how the fire had started. "I've no idea," the principal told them. "Perhaps someone dropped a cigarette."

Some nights, the woman rode up and down the Nazareth-Tel Aviv bus line. The bus driver never asked her for money.

Every now and then, before closing, she'd sit at one of the tables outside the coffee house, the one farthest from the others, staring into space like everyone else.

Night workers would see her walking through the village, round and round for hours at a time, mumbling to herself in her raincoat.

She'd wear that coat on all except the hottest nights. One summer night, she was spotted on Hamigdal Street wearing nothing at all.

Mostly, people saw her as they crossed the empty lot behind the post office. She'd be sitting on the grass tending to birds with broken limbs, humming to puppies or newborn kittens abandoned by their mothers.

Yet, for the most part, the woman seemed shy of daylight. She never asked for money, refused all offers of food, turned away when people spoke to her, and disappeared by morning.

Mr. Lazamof snuck back into his house in the small hours of one wintry morning to find a puppy in his left slipper, tiny and in need of food. A week later he almost fell over a kitten as he came out of the bathroom. It must have been in a scuffle of some kind because its right ear was torn.

"What is that?" Mrs. L asked him.

"Nothing." He took it out to join the puppy in the shed.

A series of birds were found after that, one with a broken wing, one with a missing leg, another gasping for water. Mr. L left a note for Hannah with her plate of food.

"If you come out of your room, I'll help them."

That was the end of the animals. Every night after that, Mr. L slid a note under Hannah's door.

"Write to me."

No response.

"Please, my Hannah'le, write."

Not a word.

"Tell me what you want, anything. I need to hear from you." Nothing.

"Okay. Leave your creatures with me, as many as you want, I'll look after them."

Silence.

"Hannah'le, send me instructions. Tell me what you want me to do. Anything." He stood in the hallway above the stairs, his forehead against the door. "Please, my, sweet one, forgive us."

No note. No answer.

Mr. Lazamof went back outside to his shed. He sat till morning on his chair, holding his chest against the pain.

———∘∘∘⦿∘∘∘———

Noam and Michael sat by their stepmother's deathbed and watched their father climb up and down the stairs. By the time Mrs. L died, they'd seen enough. Their father, the brothers claimed, needed rest.

Michael insisted his father couldn't live that way anymore.

Noam told him he "thould thleep downthtairth."

Mr. L yelled at them, "Who the h——l appointed you parents over me? He stomped out the kitchen and slammed the door. Didn't come back till the following day.

"Where were you?" Noam asked as his father walked in the door. "We looked everywhere."

"It's none of your darned business where I was, who I was with—or what I did when I got there."

Noam located Rosa through a cleaning agency and mailed her instructions while Michael arranged for her payments. For three years following the death of Mrs. L, Rosa arrived at the Lazamof house early each morning, sent Tikvah and her lunch off to school, and carried Hannah's tray up to her room—in that order. She'd go back to her own home, which was only two streets over, each afternoon, and return late each night after the granddaughter had gone to bed. Every night Rosa climbed the stairs carrying Hannah's food tray, and every night Mr. Lazamof trailed behind her clutching the banister like an ancient child.

Weekends and holidays, Mr. Lazamof handled the deliveries himself, reverting to his boiled chickpeas and his daughter's bird magazines.

For three years, Rosa stood witness as Mr. L hung his head outside his daughter's door, pleading with her to come out. Until one Wednesday in spring, Mr. Lazamof's heart failed him and he fell down the stairs like a bird from the sky, his life clicked off. On Tuesday, he was outside in his shed. The radio was playing army songs and he was gluing together pieces of a broken saucer. On Thursday, his family and neighbors were burying him next to his wife.

Rosa was divorced, childless, and cured of all romantic aspirations. She moved in.

"You'll stay home, Tikvah. Children don't go to funerals."

"My grandparents are dead. I decide for myself now." Rosa turned her back, went about her business.

Tikvah waited, then traipsed after her. "Don't be mad," and she tapped Rosa on the shoulder. "Mr. Lazamof is my grandpa. Even if he's dead, he's my grandpa. I need to be with him when he goes up to heaven."

Noam drove them to the cemetery in his new blue Ford. Tikvah climbed in the back, next to Rosa, hoisting a brown paper package onto her knee.

"What's in your package?" Rosa acting again as though she owned her. "You won't need anything at the cemetery."

"I'll need this."

"Sweetness, perhaps you should leave it at home."

"No, I need to take it with me."

It was a cold Friday morning. The sky hadn't yet chosen its color. Silence hung like a dust cover over the cemetery, pierced only by the chirping of finches in the pines. Plot number 7 was where they had gathered. Plot number 7 was where her grandpa was being "interred."

Many of the tombstones had crumbled with age, while some graves were so fresh the stones had not yet been laid. The earth on those graves was moist, newly turned. Ready for planting, Tikvah thought. She muttered a quick prayer under her breath—because if anyone hung out at cemeteries, it must be God—that her grandpa, the agnostic, wouldn't sprout leaves or branches as punishment for not believing, that he wouldn't grow into a tree.

Stones had been left on the surrounding graves, promising in their own pathetic way, Tikvah realized that Mr. L's graveyard neighbors were not forgotten. A desert wind blew gravel and dust against the mourners' faces as they gathered around Mr. Lazamof's hole. They could hear rumbling in the distance, gunshots on the border.

"You can leave your package on that bench, if you like."

"No. I need it with me."

"It's heavy. It will be too awkward for you to hold." Tikvah didn't answer.

They waited in silence, together with all their neighbors, at the side of Mr. L's hole.

"Rosa."

"What?"

"What's that black car?"

"That's the hearse. Speak in a whisper, sweetness, they're starting the service."

A box was being carried from the hearse to the graveside, draped in black. It took ten men to carry it.

"Stand close to me. Hold my hand."

"The grave's too small for him," Tikvah pulled on Rosa's elbow. Rosa didn't answer.

"Rosa!"

Rosa was reading from the little psalm book they'd handed out at the entrance to the cemetery.

"Rosa! They can't bury him in there. The hole's too small!"

"Hush, sweetness, not now," and the housekeeper wound her arm round Tikvah's waist.

Tikvah knew who the rabbi was. He was the one leading the service. Noam and Michael were standing next to him pretending to read the prayers. Tikvah pulled away from Rosa. She elbowed her way through the neighbors, her bundle knocking into people's knees as she passed.

"Rabbi!"

She tugged at his sleeve.

"Rabbi, this is important!"

"What is it?"

"That hole is too small for Mr. Lazamof."

"No, it's the right size. Hold my hand," and with her left hand firmly in his, and her right hand clutching her bundle against her stomach, the rabbi continued chanting. She waited, shifting her weight from one foot to the other.

"There's a bathroom near the washing area." Obviously, the rabbi had kids of his own, but she remained by his side. The ten men lifted the coffin from the ground and lowered it into the hole.

"Is my *saba* in that box?"

"Yes, that's his coffin. That's where his body will rest from the journey of his life."

Noam and Michael stood by the box in which their father was being placed to rest from the journey of his life, and chanted the prayer for the dead. Rosa blew her nose, and everyone else sniffled. The service came to an end.

But I haven't said good-bye.

One by one the group of mourners approached the grave. With a deathly thud, the first clod of earth hit Mr. Lazamof.

"No!"Tikvah dashed to the head of the line. She yanked the shovel from

Noam's hand.

"You can't do that," her blue eyes brimming with tears. "My *saba* is in there!"

Her bundle unfurled. It fell from her hand. A red scarf, a man's waistcoat, a silver pocket watch, two white-tipped shoes, and a round leather cap fell into the hole.

No one moved. Not a sound.

"You can't bury him in there, the hole's too small!"

A hush, even more scary than before, descended on the mourners. "What if he's not really dead? What if he wakes up?"

In the stillness, as everyone watched, Tikvah squatted on the mound of earth that was waiting to be dropped onto her *saba*—then she slid over the edge. The mourners gasped as Tikvah lay on top of the coffin, in the grave, as she curled herself into a ball among Mr. L's shoes, his waistcoat, his silver watch, and his turd-like cap. They watched as she sucked her thumb, as tears dropped onto her grandfather's box.

Not a sound was uttered, neither a cough nor a protest. The breeze stood still. The trees stopped their leaves from rustling. The finches above held their breath. Rosa elbowed her way to the graveside, lowered herself into the hole, gathered Tikvah into her arms, and rocked her like a baby in the grave. "You shouldn't have come, sweet one. Funerals are not for the pure of heart."

On their way home from the cemetery, Rosa announced that a strange woman had appeared in their house that morning and would no doubt be waiting for them when they got home. Rosa said the lady was "next of kin."

"What does 'next of kin' mean?"

"It means she's related."

"To whom?"

"To Hannah."

"Who's Hannah?"

Rosa didn't answer.

"Did the next of kin and the Hannah woman come together?"

"I don't remember," and Rosa looked away from her, out the window. There was no Hannah when they got back from the funeral, though the

Sarah woman was in the kitchen, her skin white as chalk, listening to swing music on their radio. Her legs were propped against the sink and she was painting her toenails purple to match her jacket.

"Why didn't you come to the funeral?" Michael asked Sarah.

"Didn't have time."

"Why didn't you come when Mrs. L died?"

31

"Couldn't get away."

"Why have you come now?"

"Felt like it."

Rosa prepared a meal of salads and cold meat. Sarah sat with them, barely eating and refusing to talk. Tikvah knew for certain Sarah was related to Mrs. L by the way she never listened when she spoke to her, by the way she refused to answer, or even look in Tikvah's direction, though all she'd asked was that she pass her the paper with the black bordered notice:

"Baruch Lazamof, Beloved father and grandfather... Blessed be..." When they were done eating, when they were finished with their tea, Sarah said, "I tried to persuade Hannah to come out of her room." She still wasn't addressing Tikvah.

"And?" Noam asked.

"She wouldn't answer me."

One after the other, the adults placed their coffee glasses in the sink and climbed the stairs. Tikvah followed them. They stood at the top for a moment, huddled too closely together, Tikvah thought, no one talking. Then, "I don't know about you," Michael said, "but I've had enough drama for one day." Tikvah shrank against the wall. She knew he was referring to the way she'd behaved at the cemetery. No one moved. No one talked until Michael knocked on the door.

"Hannah, open up."

And that's how Tikvah learned there was a woman called Hannah in the storage room.

∞•○•∞

Tikvah couldn't fall asleep, so Rosa sat on her bed like a mother would have done, Tikvah realized, though she didn't know whether her own mother had ever done that. Tikvah was grateful. She knew Rosa was trying to be nice. *But let's face it*, she thought, *I'm not the one being smothered in a hole in the ground. It's Mr. Lazamof we should be sitting by, not me!*

"How can my *saba* go to heaven if he's locked in a box?"

"It's his soul that goes to heaven, sweetness, not his body."

"What is that?"

"What?"

"A soul."

Rosa sighed. "Well. It's all the things you can't do with your body: It's what you feel with, what you love with, what you want things with, what you make music, art, or dreams with, what you hurt with, like you're doing now."

"Oh."

Rosa tried again. "What is it you loved about your *saba*?" "I loved that he talked to me." Rosa waited.

"That he listened when I talked. I loved that he cooked feta cheese with rum and served it with olives, minted lemonade, and candy-covered raisins. He said style doesn't abide by rules, it allows you to choose whatever you want from the bounty life has to offer. That's what he said."

"Mr. Lazamof cooked?"

"Yes, he'd cut a half tomato into a flower and place it with a flourish of his hand on my boiled egg, next to the chicken paste he'd taken from a can, like this."

"What else did he do?"

"He had a silver dish, dented at the edges from falling so many times on the stone floor. He filled it with dates, set it on the coffee table, and I'd say, 'Are you waiting for guests?' And he'd say I was his guest. 'Would you do me the honor?' is what he'd say. Then he'd place a second napkin over his arm and lead me to the table as though I really was what Mr. L called me: his 'Queen of Sheba,' and when Noam and Michael came, which was always a celebration, he'd take his four red and amber wine glasses and a bottle of schnapps from their wooden cabinet. 'You can have lemonade in the same glass as our schnapps glass because we're a team,' he'd say, 'but you don't need to drink this stuff,' referring to the schnapps, 'because it's poison.' I'd drink the lemonade and he'd drink the poison 'to life' with his sons and me.

"This is the way it went: He'd sip his schnapps, pause with his elbow still poised in the air, look at me and say, 'Well, you'll need to take a sip, just a tiny sip. This is a celebration after all.' I'd gulp the poison down. It burned my tongue, my lips, my eyes—until I spat out the taste that was left. Michael thumped me on the back and we all laughed. My *saba's* eyes crinkled at the edges when he laughed. I loved that.

"We were standing in a group behind Mrs. Lazamof's chair as she snored in her sleep. We should have been paying more attention because she died not long after that—poisoned herself with the doctor's pills and my *saba's* arrack—and we had to get used to walking round her empty chair."

"Do you miss Mrs. L?"

"Mrs. L. doesn't need me to miss her. I miss my *saba*."

———◦◦◦▪◦◦———

Michael was talking to the door. "You can come out now. It's three years since Pnina died of sorrow, and my dad won't be standing outside your room any longer, begging like a dog."

Two minutes passed in which no one talked until Michael. "You can die in there yourself now, for all I care."

"No,"Tikvah begged. "Let her come out!"

Noam took over. "Pnina and Baruch—you've killed them both." No answer.

"Open the door, you bitth." And Noam kicked it. When there was no response, he lowered his voice, "You could never have met a thweeter man than Mr. L, and you've killed him." He leaned his head on his arms against the top of the door, kicking again at the base with his boot like an overgrown kid. "He'th dead, you've murdered my dad."

Silence.

A voice seeped through the door in a hiss of breath, "What happened?" like a ghost, like a snake, thought Tikvah, rising from an invisible basket. Tikvah's body froze. There was a woman in the closet who'd murdered her grandparents, her beloved *saba* and her Mrs. L.

Her skin was tingling all over her body. She needed time to think, but Michael and Noam weren't waiting for her to understand.

"He'th dead, we're telling you!" though it was almost certain that Hannah didn't hear Noam because his voice was choked and buried in his chest.

Noam blew his nose. He took a deep breath.

"In the name of whatever your weird mind believth in, open the damn door!"

"No!" This time Tikvah set her hands on the door, stuck her rear out behind her, and pressed forward with all her force, "No! Keep it locked!

Don't let her out!"

Silence.

Tikvah lowered her voice to a whisper. "She's a murderer. She'll kill us too."

"Suit yourself, stay in there and starve for all I care." Michael was speaking only to the woman on the other side, ignoring Tikvah—Michael, the one person besides her *saba* who listened when she talked. "I'll not leave as much as a crumb in front of your room. Ever."

They could hear rustling inside, but Michael didn't stop. "If you don't come out, if you won't pull your weight around here, if you don't act like a fully functional member of the family, you can die of hunger! You can stay in that room and rot! We're done with you!"

Member of the family! She murdered my saba and my savta!

Rosa lay on Tikvah's bed for a while after that, in silence, a sliver of a moon glowing through the curtain, lighting the shadows of their room.

"I mean, my grandmother never wanted us. Anyone could see that. How could she leave my grandpa after so many years? My *saba*, the sweetest man on earth?"

Rosa didn't say anything.

"Every day at 5:00 p.m. he did his crossword puzzles."

"And what would you do?"

"I'd answer his questions: 'What makes clouds form? How do bees make honey? Where do ants carry the crumbs they find? When did the Arabs and the Jews stop getting along?' If I got that last question right, I'd hit the jackpot. If I told him *why* it is that Arabs and Jews don't get along, I'd get a bonus point."

"Did you get those answers right?"

"Never. When I asked Mr. L for the answers, he said, 'No one even remembers.'"

"What about Mrs. Lazamof? What would she do?"

"Knit. My *saba* brought her food to her chair. She slept a lot."

"You see? This is how we keep our loved ones alive. By remembering." Each day Tikvah remembered more of what she'd liked about Mr.

Lazamof. She didn't try to remember Mrs. L. Mrs. L had left sweet Mr. Lazamof, who'd kept the windows closed and carried food to her crumb-riddled chair for a hundred years and more, who'd never complained. Not once.

She closed her eyes and saw her grandpa. It was that easy. The day the shivah ended, Monday, it was, after the others had left her at home for another trip to the cemetery, after they'd returned home and paraded ceremoniously down their street and back again with her and their rabbi, she spotted him.

She was walking to the park on her own this time because there were too many people in her house talking too much, moving things around too much, sitting in Mrs. L's chair—and she saw him. "That's Mr. Lazamof!" and she dashed after him to the other side of Razieli Street, causing a truck driver to screech his wheels, honk his horn, and yell that she should be using the crossing and does she want to get herself killed.

She paid no attention. The only thing she could keep in her mind at that moment was *That's him, that's my grandpa, the one man in the world who treads heavier on his left foot than his right when he walks, who thrusts one shoulder forward as he moves as though pushing a door against the wind.*

She was one hundred percent sure it was him walking in front of her down Razieli Street, his handkerchief sagging from the pocket of his shorts, his flag of surrender. Mr. L was wearing short pants, which was strange, Tikvah thought, because it was winter and cold out. Yet then it came to her: *That's it! That's proof! Dead people don't feel summer, winter, or clothes, because they're dead.*

She ran to catch up to him. "Mr. L! Stop! *Saba*, turn around! It's me, Tikvah!" But just before she reached him, he changed into someone altogether different, into a man with crinkly dark hair and glasses. Transformed himself completely and disappeared into the souk.

He did that every time she saw him. Each time he changed into a different person. She began to suspect that Mr. Lazamof's soul was not as friendly now that it was hopping from one stranger's body to the next, or that perhaps it was confused. *Perhaps he couldn't see well, or not at all, now that he was dead. Anybody will tell you that dead people can't see. Or hear. He's not interested in knowing me now,* she thought, because before long he stopped appearing altogether on Razieli Street.

Next, his face stopped coming to her when she closed her eyes. At first she tried to force it, to envision his features one by one: the way his nose was short and flared to the sides at the nostrils, which was why Noam claimed that Mr. L had inherited his nose from the Russians. She closed her own eyes, made herself see his, which were green like the sea before a storm. She listened for the way he clicked his tongue to dislodge food stuck in his teeth. She saw how the sinews stood up on his forearms as he worked outside, in the shed.

After a while, even that failed her. Mr. L was fading. She could no longer hold onto him. A lump developed in her throat that hurt so much it prevented her from swallowing. In the middle of doing her homework, or taking out the garbage for Rosa, or sitting on the school bus that took her from her village to school, she'd realize that hours or days had gone by without her being able to conjure him up; her lungs went on strike, refused to do what they were meant to do with regard to air and bodies that were still alive.

—∘∘⊙∘∘—

Noam echoed Michael. "Yeah, either come out, or thtay in there and rot."

"Please," By now Tikvah was sobbing. "Don't let her out!"

No one was listening to Tikvah.

The lock turned. Hannah was a big-boned woman—as tall as Noam, maybe taller—with frizzy hair down her back that was dry and colorless, a face as gray as the unpainted walls despite its freckles, and the emptiest, most watery blue eyes Tikvah had ever seen. She was standing in the doorway staring down at Tikvah, causing her to shiver suddenly from cold. The woman's nightgown was torn at the hem, her feet were bare; her toenails, like the beaks of several birds, hooked over and pecking at the floor.

Tikvah's body went from shiver to tremble, then it shook so violently she began to spasm; the woman two feet away from her had killed Mrs. L. How? Had she snuck into their house while she, Tikvah, was riding the buses looking for the pharmacist and Mrs. L's medicine? Had she killed her then, before she or the others got back? She'd killed her grandpa too. When?

The woman was staring at her, only at her. She was extending her bony arms in her direction, though clearly she was too weak to move. Still, it was obvious: she, Tikvah, was her target.

Tikvah wanted to run away, to cry, to go back to early that morning before Hannah existed, when that room was a storage closet. But she couldn't move, was riveted to that spot above the stairs, unable to blink, unable to take her eyes off the specter in front of her. *Who is this woman, why is she extending her arms to me, and what is she doing in our house?*

She wanted to know, but she didn't dare ask. Not yet. Not then. All she could do was stare at the woman's toenails, coarse, curved over, and gray— ten parrots' beaks clutching for help at the bedroom floor.

Without a word, the woman toppled over. Rosa caught her, and with the help of the brothers carried her back into her room, which was not at all a storage closet and which smelled of sleep, sweat, and filthy bedclothes. Rosa called for Noam to bring hot tea with honey, and Tikvah, soap and water from the bathroom and the giant scissors from the kitchen drawer. Sarah fled like a terrified deer to the downstairs bedroom, slamming the door behind her.

—∘∘◖◉◗∘∘—

In general, during those weeks, air was in short supply. It emptied out of her classroom. Thursday afternoon in early spring. History class. The windows were open. A beautiful day by all accounts, Tikvah could see that, a beautiful spring day without air. Her teacher was droning on about the virtues of ancient Greece while she, Tikvah, who used to be enthralled by tales of bravery, death, and what her *saba* called romantic despair, was sliding onto the floor in a flat-out faint because she couldn't breathe, because she couldn't wait, because her parents had preferred to die with each other in the desert than live with her, because her grandmother hadn't loved her enough to stick around and watch her grow, because she wanted her *saba* back then, that afternoon, that moment.

Mr. L's face was gone. Instead, others popped up: Rosa's; the youngest Hakim grandbaby's from two doors down with his slanty eyes, his pacifier stuck in his mouth and his drool; Sarah, the weird chalk-skinned woman who'd turned up on the day of Mr. L's funeral claiming she was next of kin; even she popped into her head, refusing as she did every day of their real life to talk to her, running outside, as she'd done that very morning, whenever Tikvah walked into the kitchen.

Worse. The things Tikvah had loved about her *saba* were so overused now by her memory that they'd lost their power. *I must think of him stronger. I must. When I no longer remember him, he'll be dead.*

For sure, the mourning process afforded Tikvah no comfort.

They were sitting shivah downstairs, which Michael told Tikvah is the way you mourn someone. Tikvah didn't think it necessary to comment, so he explained, "Mourning is what you do when someone you love has died." Still, she said nothing. *What's there to say?* is what she wanted to know, so he walked away from her throwing his hands up to the ceiling, asking himself out loud how anyone could have left "that sweet little girl" to those "old crazy people," though she wasn't little anymore, no one was there to hear him but her, and, in her book, no one was crazier than relatives who let a killer out of a closet to wash her hair and manicure her nails.

"I can't believe she doesn't know this stuff,"Michael was telling the walls of his father's home. "Didn't they teach her anything?"

The woman's bedroom door was no longer closed. Rosa had cut her hair in jagged edges around her face. Tikvah watched her from the doorway. *Scary, no one would know she's a killer if her hair were not so dry, if it were not for her bloodshot eyes and scaly skin.*

Rosa brought the woman down to eat with them—for sure they'd all lost their senses since her grandpa had been killed. It was plain inconsiderate of Rosa, Tikvah thought, to bring her *saba* and *savta's* murderer to the table. Clearly Hannah didn't know how to talk, and no one else knew what to say when she was around.

Rosa led Hannah upstairs again when Noam and Michael had finished shoving food around their plates. Tikvah and the others went back to their low stools and their mourning.

But Tikvah needed to talk.

"Noam, who is she?"

"Who'th who?"

"The woman upstairs."

"What do you mean?"

"The woman in the storage room. Who is she? Why is she in this house? Why did she kill Mr. and Mrs. Lazamof ?"

Noam said the woman was related to Mrs. Lazamof, and why could Tikvah not get it—"That room above the thtairth ith not for thtorage, wath never for thtorage. It'th a bedroom."

"Was she Mrs. L's sister?"

"No."

Things continued pretty much in that confusing, scary manner, except that Tikvah was too frightened to fall asleep at night, so she sat on her chair till morning with Mr. L's shovel in one hand, his flashlight in the other, and her door locked.

It was Saturday morning. Tikvah opened her door, groggy and shivering with fatigue, wanting more than anything to climb into bed—to hell with her fear—now that the night had passed.

Hannah was there. Right there, opposite her, in her nightie, cross-legged on the landing, still as the sphynx in Tikvah's history book. She was staring directly into Tikvah's face. Her colorless hair. Blotchy skin. Her milky blue eyes. Tears were blurring the features of her face like watermarks on a water jug—exactly like grubby finger stains on their water jug downstairs—causing Tikvah to catch her breath. She hadn't expected Hannah to be sad. She'd expected her to be evil.

Tikvah didn't know how long she stood on that landing without breathing, her back, arms, and hands splayed against the door that had, that instant, closed behind her. Slowly, she knelt next to Hannah. Carefully, she stretched her arms around her neck. Ever so gently, she hung her head on her shoulder. Hannah neither moved nor spoke. Tikvah waited, then helped her stand, walked her back to her room, eased her into bed. She went down to the kitchen and brought Hannah milk with bread and cheese. She left them by her bedside because by then Hannah's eyes were closed.

It hadn't occurred to Tikvah that people who killed other people could be sad. Sad people couldn't be evil.

When the first thirty days of mourning had passed, the family, such as it was, went back to the cemetery to set the stone over Mr. L's grave. Tikvah went with them this time. This time she was too tired to "make a scene."

The morning after that, on the thirty-first day after Mr. L's dying, Sarah —their strange, chalk-skinned guest—sat next to Tikvah as they ate.

"You can't put thith off any longer," as though Noam was continuing a conversation with Sarah, "You mutht talk to Tikvah. Now."

"Why should she talk to me?" Tikvah wanted to know. "She barely knows me."

Then, *No, Someone has to talk to me*, and Tikvah spoke up, directly to Sarah. "Who are you, anyway? Why have you turned up now, in our house, for a funeral that you missed, when I have never ever seen you before?"

Finally, the most powerful thought of all hit her: *Perhaps everything they've ever told me was a lie.*

"Are you my mother?"

Sarah placed her chalk-white hand on Tikvah's shoulder. Tikvah could see the purple of Sarah's nails glistening like old blood against her sweater. A shiver like ice-fire ran through her.

"I don't know you yet," though that's not what Tikvah had asked, "but I know Hannah. In time, you and I, we will bring Hannah back to life."

Tikvah began to tremble. Her sky blue eyes grew huge, round, and filled with tears. "Is Hannah dead?"

Pnina

Things might have turned out differently if I hadn't taken that bus ride.

It was 1933. I was living with my family in the area of Jerusalem we call Meah Shearim, which, as you might know, means a hundred gates. Mystics believe that the faithful should never leave Jerusalem, that it is incumbent upon them to guard over those gates until the Messiah arrives.

My parents, Reb Zusha and Chava, raised their children according to the disciplined routine of the pious. Ours was a stucco house with a naked floor, our walls adorned by sacred books and images of the righteous and the dead. An overgrown bush of indeterminate pedigree stood guard at our front door; the windows of our home protected against the sun, winter and summer alike, by ivory lace. My father's mornings were devoted to the study of holy texts, his afternoons to teaching, and his evenings to the manufacturing of suits and shrouds for members of his community.

"Good evening. I'm looking for Reb Zusha."

It was after evening prayers on the second Monday of a particularly hot June. My father was sitting, as always, cross-legged on his table, biting the final thread from a freshly tailored wedding suit when he saw the man at his door—an anemic-looking stranger in his mid-forties with open sandals and hair on his toes.

"I represent a group of naturalists. I've been asked to arrange a lecture for them on the therapeutic properties of biblical herbs. We are staying in a hostel in the center of town. The manager gave me your name."

My father was thrilled. His lecture, the naturalist said, would have to be delivered no later than that very Thursday, as his group was planning a pilgrimage to Masada for Friday, intending to remain several days on the mountain before journeying on. My father had promised to deliver a suit to Tel Aviv that Thursday, the one he'd just completed, its final thread clinging to his teeth. No problem, he decided. I'll send Pnina.

"You'd let our fifteen-year-old daughter wander the country by herself?"

My dad wasn't deterred by my mother. "True, Pnina has a tendency to daydream, but all in all she's a reliable girl. No harm can come from traveling on public transportation accompanied by half the population of Jerusalem."

So, Thursday morning, at the central bus stop, after waiting for passengers to disembark, I boarded a rickety intercity bus, my father's newly tailored suit in my shopping bag, carefully wrapped in brown paper.

I sat near the window across the aisle from two middle-aged women who seemed to be sharing a suitcase, and a younger, nervous-looking woman with a baby. For a while, the only other passenger was an old man at the back, with wrinkled khaki clothes and a caged chicken, spitting sunflower shells on the floor.

Within a couple of stops, a man in a suit and cap clambered on carrying a sack of flour, a bag of onions and an accordion. Further along, a man with baggy pants and a boy boarded, the man demanding at the top of his voice that the windows be opened. "Air, For God's sake, air, the one thing in this world we get for free." Some black-clad priests got on at the next stop, a class-load of kids in British school uniforms, and a bunch of unrelated people going to work. By that time the bus was so crowded I'd stopped counting.

We reached the edge of the city, and the man with the caged chicken and his almost palpable odor got off. So did the priests, the locals going to work, and the man with the groceries and the accordion. Hot air was blowing through the vehicle. The bus rattled over the narrow, snake-road that led in those days over the mountain ridge, tipping dangerously at every curve, threatening to topple into the abyss.

I was ecstatic. As the bus nosed downward, I watched the olive trees wave in the scorching desert wind, and swore the oath of my forefathers: If I don't set Jerusalem above all my pleasures...

In those days, it took over two hours to arrive at the coast. The bus belched to a stop. Instantly, I was overwhelmed by the sensual perfume of sand and sea, enthralled by the ancient, decaying smell of seafaring birds. For the first time, I heard the mysterious weeping of gulls and felt that they were calling my name. Air, hot as lava, beat over my head, causing my curls to stick to my neck and forehead, burning the blue of my eyeballs, forcing sweat to spread over the now-flushed paleness of my face and throat.

I, Pnina, my father's "gentle but reliable dreamer," was consumed by an urge to see the Mediterranean, to be near the sea, to feel its water wash against my skin.

I didn't need to ask where the sea was. I could smell it—there, at the end of the sand road, where the world ended. Within ten minutes I'd reached the beach, my feet naked in public for the first time since I was seven years old, my arms sinfully exposed, for the summer sun has little tolerance for the rules and regularities of the faithful.

I poured burning sand through my fingers, allowing it to cascade from my arms and legs. I walked along the shore, splashed the waves over my face and hair, even secretly down the now-open top button of my blouse, relishing the smell and taste of seaweed and salt, the anonymity of this open, sensual place.

It was still morning on a workday, so the beach was almost empty. Two elderly men were playing chess at a card table they'd set up on the sand. A third was lying by himself on the beach, his face buried under his hat. Three women—all overweight, all squeezed into bathing suits—were wading through the shallow water deep in conversation, blocking the sun from their faces with their upheld hands; and there, at the far end, were sweethearts walking hand in hand along the water's edge, he wearing a short-sleeved shirt and suspenders, she in a white dress, barefoot, sandals swinging from her fingers.

I bought soda and a packet of dates from a vendor, sat under a palm tree until the heat abated, then left for my father's client, arriving later than expected. A mirror was hanging in the hallway outside the customer's apartment, and as I waited for the door to open, I saw a stranger peering back at me. Her skin was glowing in sweat and in alarming shades of pink. Her hair had fallen from its bun onto her shoulder in a fuzzy brown rope, her blouse creased and damp. The stranger was clutching a wedding suit—safe, warm, and sandy in its crumpled paper wrapping. "Hi, I'm Pnina, who are you?"

My mother returned home late that night, despondent after an arduous day's work at the bank and an evening of tending to her own ailing mother. My father also returned late, elated by his lecture and by the interest that his strange audience of ideologues had manifested in the flora and fauna of his Holy Land. I told them about the package, that it had been safely delivered.

"Good! Wonderful!" My dad hugged me with his arm over my shoulders. "I have a delivery girl."

"Zusha," my mother protested, "will you have our Pnina roam the country by herself? No one to watch over her?"

But my father was adamant. "She's a good girl, she'll manage."

That night I dreamt that palm trees were growing in our bathtub, that my mother was cooking at an outdoor stove wearing nothing but a bathing suit, her hair untied and waving in the wind. I dreamt that I was driving a bus on the sand, along the water's edge, my father cross-legged on the bus floor behind me, sipping tea.

From that day on, twice a month, I boarded an intercity bus and delivered men's suits (and shrouds) to homes in or around Tel Aviv. Yet, between setting my feet on that sand-strewn sidewalk and delivering the merchandise, there was always a secret hiatus in which I, the reliable girl from Meah Shearim, was transformed into a lover of nature, of sea and sky, one who relished the touch of waves against her skin, who talked to wild birds.

You wouldn't have missed me if you'd come looking; I was there, always under the same hospitable palm tree. I never forgot to bring breadcrumbs from home for the birds that were flying overhead or strutting near me on the sand.

An afternoon in early fall, I'd just arrived, just sat down, when a group of loud, hard-laughing men and women who were rough and tumbling on the beach, crashed around me in the shade and, with much noise and ado, spread their towels, their sandwiches, and their water flasks under my tree. I got up to leave.

"Are we disturbing you?" asked a red-haired youth, his face covered in freckles, his eyes as green as the bright winter tide.

"No, I have an appointment in town."

"But we've not yet begun," as though we'd met according to plan, his voice hoarse as though he had a cold, yet strangely soft and sincere. "My name is Baruch. Baruch Lazamof. These are my friends. They'd be sorry if you left."

I sat back down. I'd never felt self-conscious before. I shoved my sleeves as high above my elbows as I was able.

"Come swim with us in the water."

"Thank you," feeling as old as my grandmother, "I'll wait here." The moment their backs were turned, I removed my stockings, banished them to the interior of my shopping bag.

For the first time ever, I saw myself through others' eyes, *What kind of clothes are these for the twentieth century? For the sun and sea of our country?* I shoved my skirt under my legs. *Look at me*—though for sure I wasn't addressing the half-naked young folk splashing each other in the waves. *I look like a crow, depressing, dour as an old woman.* I pulled at the fabric of my blouse. *How could my parents let me go out into the world like this?* Though I knew the answer to that, knew my parents believed modesty would enrich my spirit, would protect me from harm. "These clothes aren't modest," I said out loud, "they're mud ugly."

I watched as my new friends emerged from the sea, water cascading from their every limb. *Look at the colors they are wearing. How fun they are. Playful.* They were looking in my direction, moving their lips, no doubt even talking to me, but I couldn't hear what they were saying. Instead, *Look*, I thought, *they have legs, these friends of Baruch, men and women both. Tanned, naked legs exposed for all to see. Who would have believed?*

I couldn't find a word to say to these colorful people, yet I stayed, unable to leave, rooted to that spot.

For sure, *they* weren't uncomfortable. *This world*, I thought, *its expanse and its sky, this is their element.* I tried to focus on what they were saying, yet their chatter sounded more like the overhead interchange of gulls than conversation.

Then—like breath exhaling gently into air, like a pigeon landing, elegantly, ever so lightly on its rock—I let go: *Yes, I like these bare-armed, carefree people. I like that they're different from my family. I love their laughter, their freedom, their open, happy faces.*

I met them twice a month after that, each time beneath the same palm tree on the sand.

"We're from Russia,"Baruch told me. "We're Jewish Cossacks," which simply meant that they were horse-riding, hard-living, outdoor Jews who danced, men and women together in wild circles, their arms intertwined around each other's waists. I had never spoken to people like those.

One momentous Wednesday morning, Baruch brought a bag of freshly plucked figs to the beach. I muttered the blessing for fruit before biting into one. Baruch said, "It's interesting that you do that. We don't."

"Don't what?"

"We don't believe in God."

"What do you mean?"

"Just that."

"Oh," the bitten fig heavy on my tongue. "What do you believe in?"

"In reclaiming the earth from the desert, in building it up from the roots into the kind of fertile farmland that will feed our nation. We believe that with all our hearts."

I'd never heard anyone talk like that. *I should go home.* But I didn't. *I won't deal with this now. Won't mention it to my parents. Not now.*

I continued to come twice a month, as though hypnotized, until it was too late for me to turn back, until I—Pnina, the gentle but reliable dreamer— had nurtured dual loyalties within my single heart.

I began seeing my parents as I never had before: My father in his striped satin coat, his skull cap and side-curls, curls that wound around his ears and which were beginning to gray. As though for the first time, I noticed the lines at the sides of his eyes, noticed the tortured brown of his pupils, eyes, and nose both set to wrinkle upward in a sad, short-sighted smile whenever I looked at him. I watched as my father bent over his books each morning, removing his glasses to clean them, mumbling the written words to himself, scribbling notes. I listened at the door as he taught his students, all of them grouped together round the table, peering over the text with their heads, blocking out, I thought, their source of light.

I brought my father his tea and almond cookie in the evenings, when he sat cross-legged on his worktable munching on his pumpkin seeds and mumbling the ancient texts he loved so much. He mumbled while sewing the suits and shrouds that tied me to the sea. "It's not right to sit on the table" my mother was always nagging him about that. "A table is holy, like an altar. Almost." I had no idea what that meant. But I knew better than to ask.

I went more often with my mother to my grandmother's, to that house at the end of our alley and across the empty field that smelled of pain, of medicine, of death lurking in the shadows. I was fascinated by the strength of my mother's arms as, sleeves pushed to her elbows, she massaged her own mother's limbs, bathed her bedsores in iodine and calamine lotion, and turned her on the mattress. "When I was small," she told me, "my mother did the same for hers."

I watched as my mother prayed in the corner of the room that my grandmother be healed body and soul, wondering for the first time what it must be like for her to have her hair permanently covered, wondering whether it itched, whether in the secret of her heart my mother wanted to remove her kerchief, to walk around free and unencumbered like Baruch's friends on the beach.

Obsessive thoughts such as those kept repeating themselves inside my head as I averted my eyes from my ailing grandmother and watched my mother pray.

My mother's praying was different from the prayers my father muttered morning and night. For one thing, his were more like a truce between two old men so defeated by each other they'd laid down their arms, condemned to repeat the same argument over and over, those two combatants, with no compromise in sight.

It seemed to me that my father's prayers were more general than they used to be, that he stuck to what was safe now, praying for the well-being of the House of Israel and for all mankind. I became more and more fidgety as I considered these things until I relinquished myself to the ache that was pulling at my chest because I knew. I knew. My father's prayers were for Yossy—always and only for Yossy, sweet lost Yossy, my brother.

My mother's prayer was focused like a steamroller on the world we lived in, aimed with surgical precision at making my grandmother better, though it was eminently clear to anyone who dared cross that threshold that my grandmother was beyond help. I grew increasingly detached watching my mother pray. Didn't she want to be pretty? Because I'd watched her in the privacy of our home, and I knew she was beautiful with her hair uncovered.

I knew not to ask. What empty-headed person would even have such thoughts? Besides, I knew my parents would say that prettiness is not an attribute we value. *Why not? Sarah in the Bible was beautiful. So was Rachel. The entire fate of Israel hung on the balance of Queen Esther's beauty. Baruch loves that I'm pretty. He's always telling me that. I like that he thinks that. I like it a lot.*

My mother was kissing her tiny book now, signifying that she'd come to the end of her prayer. I watched her. *What would happen, if—God forbid—I broke the chain of daughters praying for their parents' health in rooms redolent of death?* For the umpteenth time I thought it would be easier if my brother were here, if he hadn't cut his side curls and run off to fight.

One morning, kicking the fall leaves on our way home, I asked my mother, "How do other people live?"

"What people?"

"Other people. Not like us. How do they live?"

"I don't know. "We're not other people."

"What would you do if you met them? If you had to talk to them?"

"Who?"

"Other people."

"I do meet other people, every day, at the bank."

"What do you say to them?"

"What do you think I say? I say hello. I ask them how they are, what I can do for them. I wish them a good day when I'm in the mood. Why?"

"They look nice. Other people."

"I'm sure they are nice, Pnina."

After five minutes, walking uphill in silence, my mother snapped. "What are you telling me, Pnina? What other people are you talking about?"

"I don't know. People on the streets, I guess, on the buses. People who are building the country."

"Our country is built up of all sorts of people, Pnina. That's the way the world is."

"It's nice, nice that that's the way the world is."

That night, the sliver of light beneath my parents' door remained on until 2:00 a.m. I could hear my parents whispering on the other side of the wall.

A year passed during which I learned everything there was to know about Baruch. I memorized the Russian songs he hummed as he plucked the grapes from their vine or hacked the sunflower heads from their stalks. I became familiar with the way he used the knife hanging from his waist to rip corn from its staff, grew accustomed to the impetuous manner in which he made his friends bite into his crop at that moment, at its most fresh, its juiciest, regardless of whether his friends were tossing their own produce onto the back of their truck at the time, or wanting to remain asleep in the shade until the evening hours rescued them from the heat.

I learned to recognize the cord of Baruch's forearm and the way he clenched his teeth while building his house. Before long, I was familiar with his bursts of temper, with the frustration brought on by carelessness, by leaving the crops in the field until after the frost set in, or by failing to bring the goats back in time to their fold.

I was no longer frightened by the bouts of self-doubt and despair that caused him to absent himself from others for days at a time, emerging uncharacteristically silent, almost shy.

I saw his determination—more than anything else, his insistence on building a country and a nation out of sand.

At night, among the shadows of my parents' home, I dreamed that I was clinging to the end of a rope, trying with all my might to hold on, not to let go, not to fall from my whitewashed room down, down, through what must have been a hole in the floor into the depths of an ocean, which I could see from my rope was the brightest of greens.

The floor around the hole was strewn with books, with stained fragments of parchment and with the boiled chickpeas my grandmother used to munch on, all spilled from their upturned bowls and dropping in clusters down, down into the sea beneath the floor. As I clung to my rope, I saw my grandmother lying among wine-stained pages, saw my mother too, standing with her back to me, praying from her little black book, my father cross-legged on his worktable, pulling threads from his newly sewn suits with his teeth.

It was midsummer when I left—abandoned my parents whose son had died in an alley, alone and uncomforted—walked away from my father and my mother, who'd have to suffer my grandmother's passing without me.

It was over a year since I'd met Baruch and his friends. Every moment without him was like being gagged, like waiting for someone to untie me so I could breathe.

The windows of our house were closed, shuttered against the savage sandstorm that was blowing that day across the empty lots, through the streets, into every window crack or doorway, searing people's eyes and throats.

My parents were away from home. I packed a few personal effects, some clothes, but mainly photographs of my family. I took a teaspoon from my parents' dinner set because it was engraved with their initials and I wasn't sure I'd ever see them again; I took the brass candlesticks that my parents were keeping for my wedding day, and the Bible my parents said was mine. You'd think I was going to seek my fortune in some distant land, or never to be seen again, like Yossy, my brother, who'd run off to protest the British, who'd become embroiled in a scuffle and knifed by an Arab.

I wrote a letter to my parents telling them everything that was in my heart.

"My beloved ima and aba I'm longing to come home and talk to you as I always do while drinking your special plum soup, Ima, at the kitchen table. But I have something to say that is too big for the kitchen table, something I can say only with a pen and an envelope that I can close.

"I am writing to explain for you how mesmerized I am by the sea. I know you'll hardly believe it's me who writes in this manner—I don't know whether you've even seen the sea. If you haven't, please Ima and Aba, for God's sake, if not for your own, you must. In the sea's wild beauty you will recognize God's work as clearly—I'd like to say more clearly, but I know you'll think that's sacrilege—as you do in the lines of His scripture.

"And while I'm on the subject, I want to tell you how inexplicably drawn I am to the birds, birds as gray as the predawn sky, that fly over the Mediterranean and strut along the shore, which honest to God (and I'm not taking God's name in vain) is made of spun corn, wandering inland even as far as people's rooftops. You might never have seen or heard these birds either, for I've never heard you mention them, but I encounter them when I bring your suits, Aba, to your clients in Tel-Aviv—a city dressed in white.

"You, of all people, must know how everything beautiful is part of God's world. And God's beauty sings to me when I'm near the great blue water that both separates us from other peoples and their lands, and connects us to them. For surely, strangers are walking on their beaches at the same time as we walk on ours; like us, relishing God's beauty, listening to the call of the gulls.

"I can hear you asking, Yes, but why can't she tell us that in our own home, round the kitchen table? So I will tell you that I have something else to say that is even bigger than God's birds and His seemingly calm but uncontrollable waves: My dearest ima. My most loved aba. Don't be angry. I have met an honest, moral, and loving man, and I have fallen in love with him.

"So now you're asking, How could she have talked to a man, a stranger neither of us has met, without an introduction? Then, no doubt, you'll fret and go your separate ways, blue flames darting from your eyes, Ima, and the mole on your cheek turning dark, chopping your parsley extra fast and extra finely on your wooden board while tugging your headscarf down to your eyebrows with the tips of your fingers as you do when you're mad. And you, Aba, striding round the neighborhood with your head thrust forward, your glasses threatening to fall from your nose, coming home with your book unopened, but held so tightly in your fist that your knuckles are white and your brow still puckered up.

"And all the while, Ima is holding inside her what she's really thinking—that you, Aba, should never have sent me from Jerusalem to begin with.

"When neither of you can hold your feelings any longer, you'll no doubt ask each other, 'Why doesn't she come home and tell us about him so we can inquire into his family?' But then I will tell you there's no point in your inquiring into his family because this honest, moral, and loving man does not know God.

"Now, I know you will put your head in your hands, Ima, and groan, and your face, Aba, will become ashen gray and you'll start to cough so Ima will lift her head, worry about you, and stop groaning. You will tell me there's no such thing as such a man, and that if there were I should keep far away from him. But there is, and I can't. I have met him and I love him. I love his sons too, because he has the nicest boys you will ever meet—one five, the other seven, who live mainly with their mother.

"In short, I'm writing to tell you, my dear, most beloved parents that I want to marry Baruch Lazamof and live on his agricultural farm toward the north of the country. I want to learn to milk goats and sheep, to transform the milk into cheese, to turn olives into oil and beehives into honey. I want to learn how to plant and till the soil, to build up this country that has spread its beauty like wings around me, for I have come to realize, my dear, wonderful parents, that that is the reason God has set me on this earth. If you can find it in your hearts to let me do this and come to my wedding, I will be the happiest of women. If not, I will remain forever, from a distance, your own..."

After that, silence. No answering letter. No request to come home. In any case, I was scared to return to my parents' house, frightened I'd told them too much, that I'd find nothing more to say. "We should go to them," Baruch said. I insisted that we wait.

I stayed with Annyush and Micha, Baruch's neighbors and my own new close friends. I wasn't sure what I was waiting for, but I knew we must wait.

A month passed. Two. I moved to live with Baruch in his hut. "They don't deserve this," Baruch said again. "We need to visit them."

That night, in my dream, I fell off the rope. I shook Baruch awake. "Now. We must go. It's time."

It was early fall. The sun was relinquishing its summer rage. Baruch and I climbed the hill, with its thorns and its thistles, from the Jerusalem bus stop. We took advantage of the lull in hostilities to pause at the Arab village, greet the younger women in their courtyard, the grandmother on her stool. We bought pita and olives and tasted their cheeses—they wary of us, and we of them. I enjoyed the clucking chickens as I had as a child, the play of sun and shade over the stones, the donkey braying in the alley. Baruch stretched for a runaway ball as we left, threw it back to the kids.

Twenty minutes farther and we turned into our neighborhood. We walked past the vacant lot lined with its hyssop and rosemary bushes, past the grocery store strangely empty of people, even of Mr. Ralbag the owner, at that time of day, past the synagogue, to the bank where my mother worked. There, a sign on the door read, "Closed for the funeral."

I stopped as I turned into my parents' alley with its dirt road and its scruffy houses, my hands rising as though in slow motion to cover my face. *Whose is that procession? Why are my parents holding on to each other in the front row? Why is my mother's face, her eyes, so emptied of hope?*

Ten men, three of whom I recognized as my father's students, one as the rabbi, his youngest son clinging to his knee; one was the banker with the pockmarked face from my mother's place of work. They were carrying my tiny grandmother to the cemetery, carrying her on a board draped in black.

My mother patted my cheek. My father wrapped his arms around me and shook Baruch's hand. Not a word was spoken. Not during the funeral. Not after.

For a week, Baruch and I sat in the house of mourning, bringing my parents tea morning and evening, serving them food that the neighbors had brought in, I slipping pumpkin seeds into my father's pocket for him to munch on between prayers. Baruch was sent to sleep at a neighbor's. I slept in my own room, marveling at how tiny it had become. Baruch, the agnostic, was handed a skullcap and a book and conscripted into prayer; I sat with my mother and listened as neighbors spun my grandmother's story back into life.

"Don't go," my father begged at the end of the seventh day—begged. My father—his pained eyes peering into mine as they'd peered into Yosef's, my brother's, before he left. "Baruch will learn. He'll find work here. You'll raise a family."

But we didn't stay, because Baruch couldn't do that, and because I couldn't bear the pain. "We need open vistas," Baruch, unable to raise his voice above a whisper. "We need land to cultivate, goats to milk—and Pnina? Well, Pnina needs the sea."

We left like thieves in the night.

Things might have ended differently if we hadn't.

My parents didn't attend our wedding, though I waited and hoped. One windy afternoon in 1934, when Baruch was away on some underground maneuver, a man with a skullcap that kept blowing off his head walked across the field at the back of the house in which Baruch and I were living.

"Shalom Aleichem, I'm Rav Zvi."

"Aleichem shalom," I replied, returning the greeting. "Are you lost?"

It was common to see people roam the country in those early days looking for family, for a place to settle, searching for their particular mission in life, or simply foraging for food. Yet rabbis were scarce. "How can we be lost in our own land?" Rav Zvi wanted to know. He sat under Baruch's arbor of vine leaves, ate a meal of rice with pine

57

nuts, eggs fresh from the chickens, olives. He drank my mint tea and mopped his brow. "Well," when he was done, "when's the wedding?"

I ran to tell Annyush and Micha that a rabbi had wandered onto our hillside to make our love official. "What do you think?" Annyush asked. "That he came just for you?" So Rav Zvi married Baruch and me in a dual ceremony with our closest friends. He married us that evening as the sun sank into the sea, married us under the sprawling grapevine surrounded by community and friends, married us as I yearned for my parents, for the gentleness I had left behind. "Your challenge," the Rabbi told us, "is to embrace family, friend, and stranger, especially the stranger, in your circle of love. Love is the challenge of our time."

The night following our wedding, snipers snuck into our settlement and the neighbors' children were taken down to the shelter. I guarded with Baruch on the northern edge of the houses, learning, following him, doing exactly what he instructed me to do.

The night was endless, moonless, and tense. I paced with my husband along our post under the pine trees, first each of us moving in opposite directions from a central spot, then turning and walking back toward each other. Army blankets thrown over our shoulders provided camouflage and protected us from the cold. Any call of a night bird, swoop of a bat through the trees, or rustle of a creature in the underbrush froze us to the spot, our instincts taut as hunting cats, except that cats can see, can hear their target. We couldn't.

Several times during the night Baruch shouted into the darkness, calling to Annyush and Micha and to others posted farther along our stretch of wire. The others responded—there were no more than a dozen men and women along that fence—making believe that there were more guards on duty than just us. At times, Baruch and the other men and women on guard simulated the call of a jackal, an owl, or some other night creature, transmitting coded messages to our friends in the darkness. I watched, listened, and learned.

As the sky began to pale, and the air grew cold, our watch ended. We were safe—for now. The skirmish had simply moved on, endangering others like ourselves farther along the fence.

We returned to our hut in the white light of early dawn, other guards popping out of the brush at different posts, walking with us along the way.

Having lived in the alleyways and stone houses of Meah Shearim on the far side of Jerusalem's empty lots, I had loved the aggressive involvement that sun and sky had with our every outdoor moment. Now, up north, I relished the audacity of the hills, their vistas, and of course, always right there beneath us, the sea, that hypnotic body of water with its birds.

Nighttime. I lay on our bed in the house that Baruch had built, scared of the dark, listening for Baruch's horse to bring him home. I loved the smell of Baruch's mare, the sound of her neighing, the jingle of her reins. I drew the scent of straw deep into my lungs, breathed in the musty aroma of cypress and pine, relished the mountain air as it did its own breathing in and out through our window. "Please God, my merciful God," I prayed, "forgive me for walking away from my parents, please—protect them from harm."

———◦◦◦❖◦◦◦———

Nineteen thirty-five was a fruitful year. Our son, Jacob, was born during a storm in the early morning hours of winter. It was a Tuesday. My parents arrived by bus from Jerusalem as though there'd never been a day's misunderstanding between us; Father to perform the circumcision, Mother bearing pies, casseroles, and home-baked bread, sure that anything beyond the city of Jerusalem was wilderness.

For ten days, my mother hovered over me, cooed over her grandson, and boiled diapers in the tub. Rav Zusha strolled through the settlement like the proud grandfather he was admiring the olive trees, the henhouse, the new tractor, the night guard, and the inexhaustible energy of his son-in-law. The morning they left, Baruch walked my parents to the bus stop. Draping his arm across Baruch's shoulder, my aba said, "You are the strength and hope of our country. We depend on you."

Thank you, my bountiful God.

Jacob was content as a baby, fun-loving as a child, thoughtful and soft mannered as a man. Like me, he loved the sea above all else. When he wasn't at school or working with the cows, he was on his raft, on the waves.

Nineteen thirty-six, less than a year after Jacob was born, our best friends, Annyush and Micha, brought a boy of their own into the world. They named him Simeon. The boys grew to be inseparable. They shared the same playpen, the same bench at school; they raked, sewed, and harvested together; dated together—sometimes even the same girl—though dating never went that well for Jacob and Simeon because their hearts were already taken. They completed their army service in the same unit.

Hannah was born eleven months after Jacob. She grew into a beautiful girl, tall for her age, with soft red curls and blue eyes. Above all else, Hannah loved Baruch's mare, Malka. At two years old, she'd sit on the slope of their hill waiting for Malka to bring her aba home. When they arrived, she'd trot behind the mare holding tufts of straw in her outstretched arms, calling, "Malka, Malka, come to dinner."

As she grew, her love of animals broadened. She brought dead rabbits home for burial, birds with wings that needed mending, and newborn kittens abandoned by their mothers. Like me, Hannah relished her work in the vineyard, in the orchard, and in the henhouse.

As though by mail order, Annyush and Micha gave birth to a girl of their own four months after Hannah was born, and three years before Micha left Annyush and moved two blocks down their dirt road to live with Naomie Meiri. She was a chalk-white baby with a fuzz of dark hair, squinted eyes, and a dimple on her left cheek.

They called her Sarah. From the moment she started to crawl, Sarah was strong-willed, spunky, and given to dark moods like her mother. She paid little attention to growing things, and by the time she was old enough to notice the village mare, the animal had been put out to graze.

A year after Sarah was born, one year before Micha deserted her, Annyush had a third baby, her second boy. Menasseh, they called him. Menasseh was sickly and soft-spoken as a child. He stayed home, had no friends, never went to school, but read boxes full of books his mother brought him from the library. Before long, he was registering for book clubs, sending away for academic periodicals. Literary and scholarly journals began showing up at their door. Menasseh read so much that by high school he was writing articles of his own.

In his eighteenth year, a full year after "the disaster," as the neighbors called it, and almost a year since his sister had left home never to return, Menasseh wrote a treatise of his own, which was published and became the first in a series. *Dreams*, the series was called. The first edition was a work of fiction entitled *Israel at Peace with Her Neighbors*. Within a month, it had become a bestseller, and Menasseh was famous.

He started going for walks. He joined the village gym, developed muscles, color in his cheeks, a voice. Three years after that, he married the director of research at his local library. Three children were born to them in quick succession.

In the predawn of each day, starting with the summer of their fourteenth year, the village children pulled on their sun-bleached shorts, their khaki work shirts, and their cloth hats, and were driven to the fields. Sarah and some other kids, Hannah and Simeon among them, were sent to the orchard.

Sarah was excited about working in the orchard. It would be fun picking fruit—all the kids together. And, in fact, it wasn't so bad that first year, though Simeon was too busy with Hannah to notice anyone else. Jacob, the person she loved above all else, had been dispatched to the chicken coop, and Daniela Meiri, her father's bastard daughter, was working in her group. Three times, the bastard girl walked by Sarah. Three times, she kicked her crate over, laughing out loud, causing her fruit to spill over and roll away, calling to her, "Whatever is the matter with you, Sarah? Can't you control your peaches?" She wouldn't stop. Goaded her at every turn.

"Amazing!" Hannah gushed riding home on the back of the open truck. "Wasn't that amazing?"

"Yeah," from the others—all of the others. "That was amazing." Sarah said, "What does amazing actually mean?"

"It means it was wonderful," Hannah, still gushing. "Don't you think? Working in the fields. It's... it's glorious. Isn't it?"

"It's farming," Sarah wasn't happy. "It's taking peaches off a tree. That's all it is. Don't you have anything else to think about?"

"Do you?"

Sarah looked at her brother. *Glowing with accomplishment, he is. No better than the rest of the pack, repeating everything Hannah says.*

The second year was worse. The Meiri girl was there, next to Sarah again, no matter where she went. "Why can't I work in the chicken coop with Jacob?" Sarah begged their group leader, but he wasn't listening to her. The kids were singing some biblical song about how "dark and beautiful" they were, but when Sarah joined in, her father's bastard daughter laughed out loud. "Whatever you do, Sarah, don't sing. Has no one told you you're tone deaf? Please, do us all a great big favor and shut the hell up."

It was noon. The trees were scratching Sarah's legs. They were pricking her fingers. The flies were stinging her, the sun scorching her skin, her eyeballs, her throat. Pulling peaches off the trees was hurting her back. She forced herself not to cry. She hated the other kids. Above all else, she hated that awful girl whose mother had stolen her father, who'd rendered her own mother joyless for life.

It was obvious the bastard girl was having fun. *I'll work late afternoons from now on*, Sarah told herself, *when she won't be here.*

No one was telling Hannah and Simeon not to sing. No one was telling *them* they were tone deaf. There they were, two rows over, cracking jokes, picking fruit, singing as though they were King Solomon's biblical bloody consorts.

Sarah kept telling herself that if Hannah and Simeon could have fun, so could she. Yet, for the umpteenth time, she pricked her finger. Tears and sweat blurred her vision. *Stop whining*, she told herself, sounding like her mother. *Shut up, and get the darned job done.*

The sun was no friend either. It rose at that precise moment, in all its cruel glory, draining her of strength.

"Here you are," and Sarah felt a hand on her back. It was Hannah, materialized suddenly from her separate section. "I was looking for you."

"Why?"

"I missed you."

They were working next to each other now, Hannah still singing, sweat dripping off her, glowing, happy as a finch on a leaf.

"What is it about picking fruit in a thousand degrees' weather that makes you people sing?" Sarah wanted to know, "Because I can tell you one thing for certain: it's not that *your* voices are so gorgeous—they're not."

"Don't be grumpy, join in. You'll see. You'll like it."

"Just tell me," Sarah persisted, "what is it that renders you, Simeon, and the rest of our mindless bunch oblivious to the heat, the flies, the scratches, and the boredom?"

Sarah sulked. She worked—but she didn't sing, told herself she'd never sing again, while for every crate she filled, Hannah filled three, sometimes four. Finally, when the sun began to wane, when, *thank the Lord*, they'd completed their work assignment and Sarah was already stomping toward the pickup truck, Hannah and Simeon happened upon a previously unseen, totally virgin section of the orchard.

Well, lookie here, they've *found a bonus.*

"Let's do these trees before we go home," Simeon, the goody-two-shoes, said, and Hannah jumped in: "Oh, yes. Let's."

"I'm leaving."

"Don't be grumpy, Sarah," Hannah, being Little Miss Goody Girl, "We'll help you."

"Oh! You will, will you? You think I need your help? Well, listen to this: You can pick peaches and sing till your voices croak and your very real and very stupid cows come home. I quit."

She didn't wait with the others for the pickup truck. She walked, six miles, all the way home. "I want to work in the sewing shop," she told her mother.

"What? With the old women?"

"Yes, indoors. With the old women and you."

So she worked in the shop, repairing torn clothes and sheets, watching the other kids leave for the fields in the mornings, turning her back to the window when they returned.

When she was seventeen, her mother sent her into Tel Aviv for sewing supplies. She got off the bus alone in the middle of the city and fell in love, in love with its business and bustle. From that day on, she hitchhiked often into Tel Aviv, ordered ices at sidewalk cafes, or, when she had no money, simply sat at a table watching the people. One day the waiter wasn't there. The cafe owner removed the soiled ashtray from her table, wiped it with his cloth, sat down opposite her, and said, "Hey. You look like a nice girl. Want a job?" She spent her earnings in the city's stores buying colored candies, lipstick, and a low-cut blouse. One particularly beautiful Monday, she was walking through the department store after work when she saw a pair of sandals: Velvet. Black. High heels. Straps.

"Beautiful, shoes that movie stars wear."

"Pretty, aren't they?" the salesman asked her. "Want to try them on?" She bought them.

A glass bowl, rounded and tall, stood on a pedestal on the counter next to the checkout counter. Exquisite. Filled with the peppermint candies she loved so much. "Help yourself," the salesman urged her.

"How much are they?"

"No charge. We keep them here for our customers before the Hanukah holiday. Take one. Drop a couple in your purse for later."

Sarah paid for her shoes. The salesman walked off to another customer. Sarah lifted bowl and pedestal from the counter and sailed toward the exit. The store was full of people. No one noticed her. The moment she was out the door her body collapsed, melted like a butter puddle onto the sidewalk. Her face was flushed. Her hands tingled. She couldn't stop her teeth from shaking. *What have I done?*

She paced round the block. For half an hour she walked, needing to move, unable suddenly to keep still. Then, *You can't leave,* she told herself, again hearing her mother's voice in her head: *You're going to have to get back in there, so shut up—and get the darned job done.*

No one saw her as she carried the magnificent glass jar, in plain view, through the store. Her salesman was no longer there. *Good. He's selling movie-star shoes upstairs.* Sarah placed the bowl on the counter and turned to leave. No one noticed. Then, "Miss!" She was at the exit. One step more and she'd be on the sidewalk, but a saleswoman was running after her, calling to her as though the building was on fire. She couldn't leave now. She'd already turned around.

"Miss," the saleswoman was shouting, causing everyone, customers and salespeople alike, to stop what they were doing and stare. A plastic smile was painted across the woman's face and she was holding the bowl like a banner above her head. "Miss, you've forgotten your bowl."

Now, people were noticing Sarah, for sure.

Sarah got the hiccups. "It belongs to the shoe salesman," hiccup. "I left it there for him."

"Oh," the plastic smile still in effect, "that must be David. His shift ended a few minutes ago. He's gone for the day."

"Yes, that's why I left it on the counter, so he'll find it there in the morning."

"So sorry, David won't be working tomorrow." A crowd had gathered.

"I'll leave it on the counter," Sarah hiccupped, surprised at her confidence. "He'll find it there whenever he comes back."

A second saleswoman joined the group, probably a supervisor.

The smile vanished. "You can't leave your belongings on the property. It's against store policy."

The supervisor reached behind the counter, "I'll call Security."

"Don't bother. I'll take the darned thing with me. You can be sure I won't be shopping in your store again." Hiccup. "Neither will my friends." Sarah walked down the aisle toward the exit, her head held high, the crowd of shoppers giving way for her, one woman thrusting her face directly into hers, shouting, "For shame, a nice-looking girl like you shoplifting, someone should call the police," and another calling out to the salespeople that it was a disgrace to intimidate such a nice young girl, that couldn't they see she needed a glass of water and that they should bring her one?

The alarm went off: a deafening, screeching wail, and Sarah ran.

Shoot! She dashed across the road, missing an oncoming car by an inch.

I've missed my bus.

She hadn't.

I made it. Her skin was tingling. Gradually, her breath, threatening at first to crack her ribs, steadied, and she saw that she was sitting in the back row, riding home, a song playing on the radio in a language she couldn't understand.

She carried her bowl of candies on her lap like a trophy, trembling all the way home.

The following morning Sarah was walking from her bus stop to work. Some of the stores, the smaller ones, displayed their merchandise out on the sidewalk. An array of scarves hung from a rack waving ever so slightly, ever so seductively as she approached. The purple, the pink, and the blue were the most beautiful, but Sarah had spent her salary on sandals.

Without thinking, neither stopping nor slowing down, she scooped all three from their hooks, stuffed them into her purse, and continued walking. Her heart was pounding so hard and so loud she knew everyone on the street could hear it, knew that her chest would burst. Her face was flushed. She was experiencing the strange tingling in her fingers she'd felt the day before. Only this time it felt good. She laughed out loud. Ran all the way up the hill.

Sarah whirled round the coffee shop that morning, serving coffee and pastries as though she were on skates. *I have a secret life*, and she laughed out loud, causing the man with the briefcase to look up from his paper. "What? What's funny?"

No one knows who I am, bringing the woman and her kid their omelet. All that day, regulars chatted about their pale-faced waitress, about the unusual burst of energy with which she brought them their food, about the way she was singing to herself as she worked as though they weren't even there. "It's love," they concluded. "Our waitress has found herself a boyfriend."

At the end of her shift, Sarah lifted a packet of cigarettes from the rack, though she had never smoked. She dropped a bag full of Hanukah donuts into her bag, enough for a celebration. She hummed to herself all the way home on the bus.

For Sarah, that first day of Hanukah was the best ever. "Pnina, just look what I've brought you," as she waltzed into our home, bearing gifts: a bag of donuts, a bowl of striped peppermints such as none of us had ever seen, and a bunch of colored scarves.

The following morning, I went looking for Sarah. "It's me, Pnina," tapping on her open door. "I thought we could sit outside here on the step, for a minute, and chat."

Who was I kidding? I'd never been good either at working my way into a conversation or small talk, so, in the event, there was no chat.

Instead, I told her straight out what was on my mind. "You know, Sarah, sweetness, in this village, we don't need colored scarves, donuts, or peppermints served up in crystal bowls. What we need is purpose. There's a reason our girls don't wear fancy shoes. What we want here is workers to get down on their knees in the henhouse, scrub out the grime, and collect the eggs. We need people to man the tractor, and extra hands to milk the cow and the goats. I could do with someone in the buttery, helping me set the cheeses so we can get them to market quicker; Simeon has to get the olives off the trees in time for pressing—and, for sure, Jacob could use help with his bees."

Sarah stamped her cigarette out with her heel. "To hell with you and your moral high ground," and she stomped away.

Months passed. On her days off work, Sarah climbed alone into the hills. "My daughter," Annyush would sigh, "my sweet lost child, roaming the hillside searching for her life." Sarah sat on a rock wearing her lipstick and her low-cut blouse, smoking her cigarettes—looking down to the sea and Jacob.

Jacob watched Sarah too, followed her onto the hilltop. "Come with me under the pine trees," he coaxed. He played songs to her on his wooden flute as to a deer in need of taming.

"Teach me to swim."

"Come."

Every evening, Sarah rode home on the northbound bus, walked down our hill, and waited for Jacob to draw her into the waves. She never did learn to swim. Two, three strokes without his help, and she'd thrash the water like a drowning kitten. "I can't. I can't stay afloat without you."

—∞•◦|◉|◦•∞—

From the start, Simeon was Hannah's great love. It was Simeon she reached for from her high chair, Simeon she crawled to before she could even walk. She shared her homework with Simeon, gathered twigs with him and her brother for the fires they built on their hilltop. She danced between him and her brother in the darkness, the flames casting light on their faces, flirted with him in the shadows, and when she grew, quietly slipped her hand into his.

"Their union is written in the stars," our neighbors told us. "Fate demands that they marry."

Hannah and Simeon were married on June 16, 1954, under the grape vine that had housed our own wedding—Baruch's and mine. Two years later, the third of June 1956, they gave birth to a perfect little baby girl. They called her Tikvah.

Yet when Jacob and Sarah called the family together, when they walked arm-in-arm into my kitchen to announce their betrothal, it was I, Pnina, who resisted.

"It won't work."

"I beg your pardon?"

"Sarah," I seating her at the table, slicing my lemon cake, setting it on a plate and handing it to her, folding a napkin and setting it neatly under her fork, "you have a dark soul."

"A what?"

"You need to know yourself. You need to have a purpose, to love life before you marry."

"Jacob is my purpose. He's my life. I love him."

"You are not ready."

"I love her," Jacob said.

"How can you know that? You've never known anyone else."

"Why should I know anyone else?"

"It's not normal not to know other women before you marry."

"It was normal for Simeon and Hannah."

"No, it wasn't."

"Yet they married."

"They'll make each other happy. You won't."

My mother thinks we should marry," Sarah said. "She thinks I'll make Jacob happy."

"No, she doesn't. She's just frightened to tell you the truth."

Sarah looked across the table into the face of Hannah, the one person who knew her innermost thoughts, and Baruch, father of the man she loved.

"I need to marry my soul mate, like you did," talking so quietly we could hardly hear her. "Jacob and I deserve to be happy too."

Hannah opened her mouth, but I stared her down. I stood up and stared her down. "No," I ordered. "Don't talk!"

"But..."

"Not a word! Not a single word!"

A scarlet blush flooded my daughter's chest, her face, the whites of her eyes, the roots of her hair. She bit her nails, something I'd not seen her do since she was little, but she closed her mouth—because I was right. Didn't utter another sound.

She let me be their spokesperson.

Sarah pushed her chair from my table. She walked away from my house. She never told her mother about our altercation. Too proud. But she never spoke to me or Hannah again.

If she had, things might have ended differently.

It was the 1950s. Marauding bands of Fedayeen were crossing into Israel, murdering and plundering. Hannah and Simeon, like their parents before them, spent the early years of their marriage on night duty. Baruch watched with them along the fence. Little Tikvah spent the earliest nights of her life down in the shelter with the other babies of our settlement. During daylight hours, Baruch built a second story over our house, planning for our family and their life.

Egypt was rattling its sabers, gathering on Israel's southern border, Nasser vowing he'd rid the world of the onerous Jewish state. October '56, Israel called its soldiers to war.

"Simeon, sweetness," Hannah told her husband, "Sarah will die if anything happens to Jacob." Her parting words as Simeon left her for the desert sands were, "Promise me that whatever happens you'll watch over Jacob, that you'll never leave his side. Promise me you'll keep him safe." You'd think Simeon was the older of the two.

I watched as Sarah and Jacob clung to each other, heard her whisper, "Don't leave me," and he, "When I come home, we'll marry."

The war lasted eight days. Each day Sarah spread a cloth on the grass patch between our houses and sewed her wedding canopy. Each day she embroidered another rose onto the whitest of muslins.

On the seventh day she borrowed four marriage poles from the synagogue, erected them between the houses, and laid her canopy over them. She spent the last day of the war creating roses out of crepe paper and twining them around the poles. She waited by her marriage canopy, sitting on the grass in her sweater and scarf. We didn't open our door, never came out of our house to look at it, yet she knew we could see her. That was satisfaction enough.

The military men who knocked on our door that second day of November, who scraped their feet on the mat so many times before stepping inside, there was no need to ask why they'd come; those men—actually, the older of the two, Corporal Adler his name was—told Baruch and me how Jacob had requested a transfer from his unit to Simeon's. "He changed positions with a fellow soldier," Adler reported, "so he and Simeon could fight like brothers in the same tank."

Baruch and I sank together onto the sofa, all four knees buckling in unison. Beyond that, we didn't move. Didn't utter a word. Didn't cry. Didn't seem to see or hear the men at all.

Adler cleared his throat. "As you know, it is against military regulations for brothers to share a tank; fate frowns on that." An aching silence had taken hold. "When their tank was hit," Adler reported, his voice low, his eyes glued to the floor, "Jacob and Simeon fell, like brothers, in the sand."

The officers perched, in the silence, on the very edge of our kitchen chairs. "They are our heroes," Adler was whispering, "brave men who gave their lives for our country." We didn't respond. Not so much as a protest, a tear, a change of position. The envoys got up to leave. The younger man bent to clasp our hands in both of his; first mine, then Baruch's. Tears stood in his eyes, ready to fall. Adler said, "The people of Israel will be eternally indebted to you." They hooked their caps back on their heads and left.

We stood up then, Baruch and I. We watched from the doorway as our messengers of death walked across the grass patch, past Sarah's marriage canopy looming ghostlike in the dusk to Annyush's joyless home.

When that door opened, Baruch sank back into his place on the sofa, his teeth chattering, his body convulsing from the cold. I fainted, flat out, on our stone floor.

Tikvah was three months old. Hannah brought her to us, her parents. She sat in my chair. She rocked her baby back and forth, back and forth, holding her so tightly I was afraid Tikvah might suffocate. For twenty minutes my daughter crooned, tears spilling from her face to that of her child, talking to her beneath her breath.

Then, she raised her face to mine. "Here I don't deserve her." She set her child, in her blanket, on my table, and walked away. Carrying a cloth bag with her belongings, my daughter climbed to the second story that Baruch had built for her, her husband and her child. She walked alone into her marriage chamber and locked the door.

End of Story.

HANOVER GARDENS

Inda

Skeletons hung along the sides of our streets, caving in over their own bodies like blind widows; soot and burnt plaster flapped from them like bats in the wind—and we left-at-home women and old men were buying what we needed with coupons.

Rain was dripping down my neck, I was plodding past bombed-out buildings we'd all treasured, and I was pissed. I'd taken a bus from the bottom of our hill to the city center to buy overdue shoes for the children in my house. *First they skyrocket prices because of the war; next they lower them to almost double prewar prices and tell you there's a sale on.*

Yet here we are—my gin bottle colliding with the shoe boxes, bruising my legs like a disembodied fist through the string bag that held them—*two years into war and the For Sale sign has not yet fallen off the pink house on the corner of Grant Street. Waiting to attract some passerby, when everyone knows there are no passersby in wartime.*

I set my purchases on the pavement and leaned for a moment against the wall. When that pink house first went up for sale, they'd asked four thousand pounds for it, furnished: marble floors and a spiral staircase, unheard of in our neighborhood, high ceilings and French doors.

Our neighbors said it had a white baby grand in the front room and lace curtains that billowed in the breeze when the glass doors were open. They said it had window seats with cushions to read on, on rainy days.

It had a garden in the back with trellised arches to marry your children under when they grow up, we should live and be lucky; a wrought iron bench way too hard to sit on till the end of such a ceremony; and climbing roses I'd love to have picked but didn't because I still thought that might be stealing.

The house was boarded up, its diaphanous drapes hanging lifeless inside while the roses in the garden bloomed and faded and bloomed again—up through the weeds, the brambles, and the rain-soaked leaves, flowering under our milky English sun, then shedding their petals in the rain.

A reality of its own that house had, even as it slept, shuttered and prematurely aging, waiting out the war.

Mr. Brody had built the house for his daughter as a wedding gift. He owned two of the largest factories in the Midlands, but his son-in-law disappeared when the war broke out—"German," my neighbors said. That explained it. Mr. Brody's daughter wasn't there anymore either, so the house stood empty.

Arthur and I asked my dad to lend us the money. We'd repay him, we promised, when the war was over, but he couldn't because about that time Dad lost what was left of his savings in the last of his many failed ventures— pigeon breeding, it was. When we found him dead on his bed of a heart attack, five birdcages were perched on his kitchen table, their doors hanging open on broken hinges. Feathers were floating over my dad like shattered particles of his ever-optimistic soul with not a bird in sight. We had to fumigate the house for gnats.

It was July 1, 1939, two months before Germany invaded Poland, two months before England and France declared war on Germany, and a whole year before the Battle of Britain began. Arthur and I met with the neighbors at Mat Morgan's grocery shop, the one we called "the pub" because Mat played his piano every evening from six to nine thirty, sold liquor by the barrel, and had pin-up girls with fishnet stockings and glossy, pouting lips throwing kisses from the walls where the tinned goods should have been.

Groceries were never Mat's concern. "It's my girls"—"my girls" is what he called the lips on the wall—"not the sardines," he said, "that keep people coming." He left the groceries for his wife to deal with, so the tins were stacked underneath the counter among the sacks of rice, imported beer, and the rat poison.

I wouldn't let Arthur hold my hand when we got to the pub. I shrugged his arm from my shoulder. Why did he have to leave that night for a war that had not yet reached us? That might never happen? Why not wait until he knew for certain? *All he wants is to march into danger and make himself a hero, with me left behind to fend for myself.*

What kind of person even thinks like that?

"It's coming for sure now," Arthur announced as we walked through the swinging doors, and I watched as he sagged against the wall in the silence, his dark skin flushing like a schoolboy caught kissing the teacher's daughter. Mr. Hughie and his cronies, who were smoking their pipes while letting their beer go flat on the counter, stopped talking and turned toward us, each emitting his own particular form of grunt.

Mr. Hughie's face crumpled like a paper bag after the sandwich was eaten, his right fist shaking as he clutched his pipe, and Mr. Sharp trumpeted into his handkerchief for what seemed like forever before pushing it back, all gooey and disgusting into his breast pocket, then shuffled off home without saying good night.

"Mister," said Mat Morgan, "we've not yet buried the Great War."

My little Billy piped up in his high-pitched voice, "Will this be a great war too, Mr. Morgan?"

"Dead certain it will, son," he answered, ringing a shiny new sixpence from the cash register and curling Billy's fingers around it, "dead certain it will."

Arthur left us late that night, saying only that he was going to look for Jacob Feld, a friend from his university years. "What's wrong with you?" I hissed at him, careful not to wake Claire and Billy. "They're wanting to drag the whole lot of us into war over there— meaning guns and bombs and certain death— and you're popping over to visit a friend?"

He stood in the hallway with his backpack and his coat.

"Don't leave me."

He left.

I can still feel the thump of the door against his back as I pushed it closed, almost shoving him down the steps. I stopped breathing, counted— one, two, three. If he didn't reach the gate by five, I'd snatch him back and hold him to me forever.

By three, he'd gone. I melted onto the floor and cried myself to sleep. I hadn't let him hug me, hadn't let him kiss me good-bye.

I remembered Jacob Feld as a thin man with wiry black hair sitting at our table on weekends, showing us pictures of a petite smiling wife somewhere in Europe, her left hand resting on the head of a toddler in a summer dress, pushing a baby in a pram. He'd gone back to them, was nabbed by the S.S.

In the time that remained before the outbreak of what we politely called hostilities, my Arthur searched for Jacob's wife. She'd been taken too. I was proud of my Arthur—honestly I was. He found Jacob's daughters: little Annie hiding from the Nazis in the home of a childless Dutch couple, and Myra in a convent under a changed identity. He sent them to live with us here in England.

One after the other, other refugees—Eva, the Ungar sisters, and Miss Berliner—turned up at our door during Arthur's absence, saying they were sent by my husband because they needed a home. You'd think I was Britain's welcoming committee. Miss Berliner came bearing a note from Arthur, from Rotterdam, a copy of the letter we'd already received. "My love, remember Jacob Feld? I promised him I'd send his daughters, Myra and Annie, out of here; that they'd play with our Claire and Billy."

Miss Berliner and the letter she brought arrived seven days after we'd already brought Annie and Myra home from the docks; ten days after Eva had knocked on my door, emaciated with blotchy skin and two missing front teeth; and two weeks after Frieda and Hanna Ungar, dour-looking sisters, accosted me as I was hauling out the rubbish bin, stodgily demanding shelter.

"Don't you have family here, Miss Berliner?"

"No."

"No friends? No one you know?

"No."

"Well, where did you expect to stay?"

A feather was perched on her hat, dark blue and shabby. Buttons were missing from her coat. A suitcase, the kind they all carry— battered beige, a life-story of stickers oozing guilt on my pavement— was perched on the asphalt beside her like a long-suffering dog I refused to look at it.

Dull eyes.

I hate feeling mean.

I took her in.

Annie Feld was five, matted fair hair, her face pale as curdled milk, scrawny as an alley cat. Myra was seven—taller, darker, with corkscrew curls and terrorized gray eyes. She stood so close to Annie it was hard to know who was protecting whom. They were dressed, courtesy of some charity, in identical gray coats and old people shoes.

I knew Myra was expecting me to deliver them from whatever disaster was lurking round the corner—I saw it in her eyes. Some days, I smelled disaster. Saw him sitting on my bureau, his legs crossed, waiting.

Please God, bring my Arthur home.

Myra never took her eyes off me. I could tell she believed in miracles by the rosary she wouldn't let anyone take from her, by the way she clenched her knuckles around it. I kept telling her, "Myra, you're Jewish. You don't need a rosary," but she clutched it like an intravenous drip. She bit her nails. At night, while she slept, she pulled her hair out. In the mornings, I'd find disconnected curls, abandoned and dark on her pillow.

Annie cried a lot at night. She wet her bed. During the day, she wet her pants. She sucked her thumb. She scratched her pink skin till it bled.

Disaster sat cross-legged on my bureau: blood-shot eyes, blue hair, top hat, striped pants—silk. He was smoking, biding his time, dropping ash on my carpet, making clicking noises with his tongue.

———∘∘◦❁◦∘∘———

August thirtieth, with no warning whatsoever, Arthur opened our front door. I clung to him like my life depended on him, because it did.

Disaster hopped off the bureau and doffed his hat. "I'll be back," and he jumped out the window.

Each night after that was a blackout. Our laundry grew into a mountain on the washing table. With a war going, it didn't seem worth the folding.

I worked at the pharmacy five mornings a week. I relished its silence, the whiteness of its walls, its blue and crimson bottles—the way the light gleamed through the bubbles in the glass. Weighing, mixing, and dispensing added stillness to my life. I'd always loved that. Now—not so.

The war was crowding into my sacred space. Switching the wireless off, even turning it down, seemed unpatriotic. So I was bombarded by war tunes left over from the last "Big One," and by declarations of "enemy aggression," "hostilities," "encroaching war," and the need to "defend our country with honor." I clamped my hands over my ears and prayed the electricity would fail.

People dropped their prescriptions off and picked them up without thinking to say hello. No more "Good morning," no "Have a nice day."

We were waiting for something to happen, someone with enough sense to come on the wireless and tell us once and for all that "hostilities" had been canceled, that all our talk about the Nazis and their practices as a self-proclaimed master race was misinformation. We were waiting to hear that our men and women who were already over there could pack up their uniforms and their various lucky charms and come on back home—that we could stuff sandwiches, best wishes, and caramels into our refugees' pockets, their satchels, and their worn-out handbags, and send them forever back where they belonged.

Four p.m. on September 7, Hitler bombed London. London! Three hundred and forty-eight German bombers and six hundred and seventeen fighter planes fell over the city. Two hours later, a second attack that lasted until the morning. London Bridge, as the song goes, was falling down.

In fact, the Germans would bomb London for fifty-seven days straight —bomb England until the following May, sometimes during the day, sometimes throughout the night.

Evenings, we huddled round the wireless—Arthur, me, and our group of foreigners, forgetting to switch on the overhead lamp until we could no longer see each other, banishing sleep as the ultimate seducer, relying on the morning paper to bare witness, Arthur translating the war reports for our guests.

I didn't cook. We pulled bread from its loaf as we listened and nibbled on cheese. Claire and Billy scurried without me through the cupboards, partying on leftover biscuits, mixing sugar into the cocoa powder, ruining their teeth, pouring condensed milk into their mouths straight from the tin.

Londoners, the newscaster told us, were carrying their bedding to the underground stations to sleep with the rubbish and the rats where they thought the bombs wouldn't reach them. All told—a hundred and seventy-seven thousand people found shelter underground.

I was in London once just after my mother died, when I was eleven, riding the underground with my dad. Now, listening to the wireless, I remembered the primordial roar of those trains; the way they'd belched like obscene beasts into the air as they huffed on their tracks. I remembered the acrid smell of metal turnstiles, tickets, and dust. In my head, I saw newspapers whipped to hysteria by wind, warm and sweet as a giant train fart, hurtled down tunnels as tiled and grimy as public lavatories.

An old man was slumped in a corner, his grisly hair wiping those tiles. As I listened with my husband and refugees to the news, I remembered the creases on that man's face, the loneliness of his extended hand, the soot, the stench of urine. Next to him, propped against the wall, was a placard:

Prepare. The End of the World Is upon Us.

I clung to my father's coat. I pulled him from that place.

City children, the newscaster was telling us, were being evacuated to the country to live with relatives or strangers. Officials, people who knew, were telling us how things would be.

It was midnight. Annie and Miriam—Myra for short—had crumbled into sleep on the carpet, Miriam with her arms around Annie, Annie in a ball, sucking her thumb.

Ms. Berliner, who could never keep still, was on her knees in the kitchen punishing the floor with a scrubbing brush for the sugared cocoa and condensed milk my kids had spilled.

Eva was ironing, gulping Mat's Take Home and Enjoy Beer out of my dead mother's best teacup.

The Ungar sisters were sitting like bookends across the card table, their feet laced in boots, tucked beneath their chairs. Frieda's fists were clenched one inside the other in her lap like a student listening to a lecture, waiting for a break in the monologue to voice her protest. Hanna was plucking the fringes out of my tablecloth, chewing her lip till it bled.

No one within earshot of the wireless was talking, but Claire and Billy were chasing each other upstairs, slamming doors, shouting to each other in their boredom, playing hide-and-seek. We'd forgotten to send them to bed.

So we knew how things would be.

Arthur resigned from his job. "I've nothing to teach, and no one to teach it to. I need to get over there and fight."

I went out back to pace up and down and bite my nails. *Please God, my peace-loving God, keep my Arthur home.*

So my husband was in uniform, dispatching others off to fight while he was forced to wait, desperate to be shipped out. Each morning, before reporting for duty, he appeared at the war office begging to be sent into action.

"What kind of man sits behind a desk while others are over there, risking their lives?"

"Relax," offering him a beer, knowing he wouldn't take it. "It'll be any day now. We'll call you."

He wasn't happy. He told me he was dragging his heels. I hung my head low over my chest. I let my shoulders droop. I turned my lips into an inverted U and circled around him slowly, ever so slowly, scraping the floor with my feet, pulling my upside-down toes like sandbags behind me. That made him smile. "You see? I've taken the wind out of your sails," and I heaved a lungful of air into my chest.

He laughed at that, a pale, anemic laugh, as panic surged into my throat, as I gulped a sob back into my chest. He pressed his lips into my hair. "How can I be happy here with you when other men are drafted?"

So he volunteered for extra neighborhood-watch duty. He collected provisions for the refugees who were housed in the school hall. He brought them tinned fish, cheeses, and blankets so often he knew all of them by name.

Arthur told me that early one morning—he'd just delivered carrots to the refugees and was walking to work—an eerie feeling spread through him that he was being followed. He said he could hear breathing behind him. He stopped and turned around. Shopkeepers were rolling up their shutters and opening their doors. Some were pulling vegetable stands onto the pavement. Other than them, no one was there, so he continued walking.

The thing that worried me most about my husband, at that time, was the intensity with which he held me through the night, and his determination to draw closer to Claire and Billy.

He started by reading them to sleep each evening, but ended up lying between their beds inventing songs and stories. "As we speak," he told them, "goblins with golden hair and translucent bodies are rising from the mountains."

"From the mountains?"

"Yes, from deep inside, under the trees, where they live during the day. They are flying over Hanover Gardens at this very moment spraying magic dust."

"What's the magic dust for?" Billy asked.

"To protect us from harm."

He sang until my children tumbled into sleep on the floor, leaving Myra silent and wide-eyed on the other side of the room, with little Annie padding across the hallway, calling, "Auntie Inda, what are goblins? What does *translucent* mean, Auntie Inda?" and, "Why is Uncle Arthur talking about fairy dust? Myra says there's no such thing."

Arthur told me he'd felt that strange sensation a second time, while walking to work. This time, he hadn't stopped before turning. A woman with a shopping bag, he said, was crossing the road; some boys were sitting on a doorstep, rolling marbles into the gutter. A peddler, with brushes and brooms, was pushing a cart up the hill. Nobody was following him, so he continued walking to work.

Every now and then, Billy or Claire (or both) came whimpering into our room at night. The first creak of the door, the first "Daddy, I had a bad dream," and Arthur's eyes snapped open like a frog on a rock. Already upright, towering above me on the pillow, he'd announce, "I'm up, I'm up, we've slept enough. Let's walk." And he was under the bed, searching for his slippers.

They padded around our neighborhood in blankets and pajamas, talking about the Milky Way and how mariners from ancient times navigated the seas.

They told me about it in the morning.

They talked about hot air constellations and watched the formation of clouds. They lay on the wet grass behind our house listening as night creatures rustled around them, Arthur telling them about the rhythm of living things and how humans are part of that chain. My children fell asleep as Arthur talked. He carried them back to bed.

Miriam and Annie kept their nightmares to themselves. When we checked in on them, they squeezed their eyes shut so we'd leave them to their pain. I sat on their bed and stroked their hair. "Talk to me," I whispered. Annie squeezed her eyes tighter and held onto my hand. Miriam wrapped her arms around my waist.

"All wars end, eventually."

"Yes, and people get killed," Miriam: pained gray eyes and an ancient soul.

"I'm making breakfast," Arthur called. What my children wanted was hot chocolate and eggless pancakes (eggs were rationed), so that's what they got: runny, formless, fantasy pancakes.

Yet again Arthur told me he'd heard breathing, short and shallow, and shuffling behind him. He'd walked a block further then ducked into a side street and peeped out. A child, no more than nine or ten, in a threadbare gray coat, was looking up at him. Arthur crouched to the curb, "Hello."

The child had turned, had raced back down the street, heaving a cloth bag over his shoulder, heavier than himself.

Arthur hadn't intended to hurt the boy. All he'd wanted was his name. Three times, the principal phoned, "Are your children sick? Why aren't they here?" Three times, the military dispatched a messenger, "Where's your husband? He hasn't turned up for work."

The first time they went AWOL, Arthur bought Billy and Claire boiled sweets and lemonade from Mat's pub, and took them to see the "funnies" at the flicks. The "funnies," Claire told me, were for Billy and her; the newsreel showing rubble, frightened people, and planes screaming and dropping bombs over buildings, was for him.

About three weeks after he'd encountered the little boy, Arthur told me he'd heard those self same breaths behind him again—panting, hurried—and that shuffling sound, which he now recognized as the child's bag being dragged over the asphalt. He told me that a couple of times he'd caught a glimpse of the boy, had even called out to him to stop, that he didn't want to hurt him. But no, each time the child disappeared.

The second time my family went missing, Arthur pulled balloons, left over from Billy's birthday, from our cupboard, blew them up and took our children on the bus to the fairground on the other side of town—which everyone knew had been closed for a year.

"Mister, there's a war on."

Arthur told me he paid the guard money we didn't have. The man ruffled Billy's hair, tipped his cap, and grinned.

"Here, flip this switch."

"Who? Me?'

"Yeah, kiddo, you. Who else?"

"Wow!"

My Billy got to turn on Fun World.

But, as the lights came up, a dog—a massive, brindled beast, saliva whipping like rope from both sides of his jaw—came charging out at them from behind the Big Wheel, barking, snarling, and baring its fangs. Claire clung, screaming to Arthur. Arthur stood his ground. Billy whipped around and raced for the exit. The guard lunged at the dog, grabbed its collar in the nick of time, threw the beast a bone from his pocket, and—who knows— probably saved my Billy's life. Satisfied with its prize, the beast crawled from the light, disappeared beneath the booking office.

Claire and Billy wanted to go home. "Does running away mean I'm a coward?"

"No, son. It means you have a healthy instinct to stay alive."

Arthur and Claire huddled with Billy for a while, shivering in the cold beneath the exit sign. The guard offered them strawberry ice cream with chocolate sprinkles, free from his freezer.

The man set the Ferris wheel in motion. He took a picture, no charge:

Arthur, Claire, and Billy suspended in a giant bubble of light on the Big Wheel, balloons bobbing behind them against the clouds.

Arthur told me that he'd just taken out the dustbin one evening when he heard a rustling in our hedge. He saw two eyes peeking out at him from the berry bush. "Come, boy," he called. "I'll give you food."

The eyes vanished. The rustling stopped.

The third time they played truant, Arthur filled my children's pockets with peanuts and went with them to the track. *How would we survive without him? I'd never do such fun things with my kids.*

It was not at all what they'd expected. Claire told me that no-nonsense people, people who were too old to go to war, were lined up ahead of them when they arrived, wrapped in scarves and gloves and stomping their feet against the cold, waiting for the booking window to open.

There were two not-so-old women wearing sweaters and shawls over diner uniforms, who had a single string bag between them. Claire could see they were scared to take their money out while people were looking into their business. But the fat woman who was opening the ticket office for business, who had purple fingernails and rings on every finger except her thumbs, told them not to worry. "Horses are big money. No one here has his eyes on your two-bit fish net."

Claire said most of the old men were smoking and minding their own business.

People coughed and sneezed as they waited in line. The man behind Claire and Billy, with wispy gray hairs over his cheeks like an ancient chicken, leaned over them, gave them horse advice, and breathed sour breath into their faces.

"Take a good look at them pictures before placing your bets. Over there by the wall. Make sure you check their teeth and eyes, 'cause one thing ole Eddy can tell you for certain—a sick horse will never run."

"What should their teeth and eyes look like, Mr. Eddy?"

"Ooh, Mister, did you hear what your son asked there? He's a smart one, he is. You should be right proud."

"I'm proud of both of them. More than they'll ever know."

The man spat on the asphalt. "Well, maybe you are, or maybe you ain't. What I want to know is why a handsome male the likes of yourself, with nothing visible wrong with 'im, ain't over there fighting the Krauts alongside my son."

And to Billy, "No moles. Absolutely no brown spots." He drew a paper bag from his raincoat and took a swig.

"Don't be staring at me like that, neither. It's tonic. It's for me bleedin' ulcer."

Arthur didn't respond. He put his arms round Claire and Billy. They checked the eyes and teeth on the prettiest horse pictures. No moles. No brown marks.

Arthur gave my children three shillings each to place on a horse. "It's a lot of money. Think before you choose."

Billy couldn't decide whether to bet on a black mare called Silver Bullet or a stallion called True. Claire chose True, and Billy said he'd go in with her. Eddy, the phlegm-spitting chicken man, steadied himself on Billy's shoulder.

"Nay. You should bet on Daredevil. He's a dead ringer."

"Don't mind him," Billy told Claire. "It's his ulcer. It makes him speak funny. It's because he's sick that he's toppling around like that."

But Eddy was right there.

"No need to whisper behind me back, lad. It's because me boy is off fighting the Krauts—unlike some other men you might know who keep right on at home with their kids, livin' the good life. It's because I'm hurtin' for me boy that I'm topplin' around."

Silence. Claire told me she and Billy didn't know how to answer the chicken man. They walked over to the board again to check out Daredevil: clear eyes, clear teeth—brown blotches all over his body.

Billy didn't know what a "ringer" was, but felt it'd be bad luck, for certain, to bet on a dead anything.

"Dad, what should I do?"

"True was the one you chose. Trust your judgment."

Arthur waited to pick his horse until Billy and Claire decided on theirs. "Choice is personal. It's like people. No two are the same."

The lady with the fingernails and the rings leaned forward till her pink hairnet emerged from her ticketing-box.

"Mister. You talking to a whippersnapper like that about choice? Before he's learned to keep the snot from his nose?"

Silence. No coughing. No spitting. Mr. Eddy with the ulcer stopped wobbling on his feet.

"He'll be finding out soon enough what little choosing there is to go around. I can promise you that for nothing and a half."

All it took for the orderly line to break into a crowd was the pink-headed woman popping out of her box. "Miss, you going to sell tickets here, or what?"

"Right you are then." Her pink head retreated and her rings popped out. "Did you come to bet on horses, mister? Or talk? There's customers waitin' here."

Arthur placed his money on Home Free.

The woman handed him three tickets and three Union Jacks.

"God save the King, next!"

It began to rain—a gentle, steady curtain. The arena was gigantic. Announcements were blasting over a loudspeaker, echoing over the bleachers against background music like a circus, only without the balloons or the clowns. It was so loud they couldn't hear the words or the music, just the noise.

Yet Claire said there was an eerie hush underneath the noise on the rows and rows of wet half-empty bleachers where they sat. "A creepy, eerie quiet" is what she said it was.

It wasn't like a holiday. The men and the two nervous women were serious, focused people. Billy said they didn't look one bit happy.

Arthur pulled my children's hoods up against the rain. "Horse betting is fun. That's why we came."

Claire said no one looked like they were having fun.

Suddenly, the fanfare began—drum roll, trumpets, announcements blasting over their heads. Everyone stood up. The men clamped their hats over their hearts, and the loudspeaker played the national anthem.

Billy thought the king was coming.

Horses were at the gate—their horses. A gun was shot, a real live gun, Billy said. Everyone was on their feet now, for certain, jumping up and down, screaming.

Arthur, my sweet, rational husband, said he thought he'd burst some vital organ following his horse, shouting its name. Claire and Billy, he, the two nervous women with the fish net, Eddy the phlegm-spitter, and all the lonely men, everyone waving flags and throwing soggy hats into the air. All were screaming instructions onto the track as their bets whizzed by—all suddenly horse-running aficionados—instructions that were in any case drowned beneath the trumpets, the loudspeaker, the now furiously falling rain, the bugles, and the drums.

Arthur said it was like the angels and devils of heaven and hell were released from their holding places, all of them together surging toward earth, rooting for the human race!

Daredevil came in first.

—∘∘◦❉◦∘∘—

Every day, Arthur left a meal outside our kitchen door—in a box with a lid, so the cats wouldn't get it.

"What's that for?"

"For a little boy I saw running round the neighborhood who's hungry." Claire told Billy, Billy told Myra and Annie. From then on, they took turns leaving food in its box.

Most times, the meals were gone by morning.

Arthur grew to like being followed. He got used to catching glimpses of the boy, his wide-shouldered coat that seemed more like an adult's jacket, his short, shallow breathing, and the dragging sound of his bag.

——∞◦}●{◦∞——

The more eager Arthur was to leave, the quieter he became, the tighter he held me at night—and the closer he drew to our children.

Me? I was betting on the war office to keep him home.

——∞◦}●{◦∞——

There were days when he neither saw nor heard the boy, and when the food remained in its box. When that happened, Arthur paced round the neighborhood, calling into the shadows. When there was no answer, he sat outside all night, listening. Claire, Billy, Myra, and Annie perched on the steps with him until he ordered them to bed.

"Something bad could have happened to him, Inda. Should we call the police?"

"What will you tell them? That there's a little boy, probably illegal, waiting to be picked up, deported?"

Two months later, with Arthur agonizing that he'd been forgotten by the war effort—and me happily deluded—he was drafted.

He climbed onto the roof and repaired loose tiles. For three days he checked the windows, the locks, and the taps. He stocked our home with enough toilet paper, licorice strips, and coloring books to last us seven wars. He made the beds, took the rubbish bins out to the curb. "Don't you lay your hands on that," I snapped, when he reached for the broom. "Don't you dare. It's mine!"

He hardly spoke. None of us knew what to say. The day before he left, we packed biscuits and sausages into a paper bag and walked to the park. We ate the sausages in the rain and fed the biscuits to the ducks. "Hey," Arthur suggested, "how about I build you a tree house when I come back?" No one answered. He turned his collar up against the cold after that. We walked back home. No one talked.

Claire, Billy, and I followed him onto the platform beneath a horn of smoke and soot, a deafening noise of engines, whistles, officious undersized porters clanging doors, pigeons that had inadvertently flown down through holes in the glass-domed ceiling and were scurrying with everyone else for all the world as though they'd lost their suitcases, and departing trains.

We were herded along with the traveling pigeons and the many other soldiers, every one of them pale-faced and glum, allowing themselves to be hugged by their loved ones, shrinking what they most wanted to say into grunts.

Arthur hugged me until I could barely breathe before boarding, but after what seemed like a single second, he was wrenching my hands apart from the back of his neck. They were probably killing him—my hands—as he was so much taller than I, but he didn't feel comfortable bending down to kiss me— he was representing England, after all. In any event, I wouldn't unlock my hold on him and he needed to leave.

"Inda, look." At the far end of the platform, alone among the milling crowd, was a little boy, a man-sized jacket sagging from his shoulders, a cloth bag hanging from his hand.

"Boy!"

The child was looking at Arthur. Slowly, he raised his right hand. Arthur raised his in response. For a moment, a group of people blocked him from sight. When they passed, the child was gone.

But Claire had her arms around Arthur's waist, sniffling mucus onto his brand new uniform, and Billy was tugging his hand down to his own height screaming at the top of his lungs because he was still so short and uninhibited and he needed to be heard above the noise. They hadn't seen the boy.

"Don't go, Daddy. The war doesn't want you. We want you more." I tugged too at his hand, "Yes, we want you more."

For a while there we had Arthur tied down like the giant in Gulliver's land of the Lilliputians. We were almost successful.

Almost, my dad would have said, had in fact said at the end of each of his failed projects: "Almost, but no cigar."

Arthur, my sweet, earnest "husband of the dark brooding eyes," as I liked to call him, left us on November 11, 1939, to our brown house on Hanover Gardens.

Disaster moved back in, brought his luggage, his newspaper, his smirk, and his top hat, set up quarters on my Arthur's chair.

"I can't do this," I told myself. I went to bed. I heard Claire and Billy, and perhaps even Myra, whispering outside my closed door. I heard the floorboards creak as they crept back down thinking I was asleep, not wanting to wake me. Then I heard the back door bang shut. It banged again, again, and again.

Now, my houseguests were clattering in the kitchen, throwing pots and pans—slinging my dead mother's crystal bowl and all my best china— against the walls.

Someone switched the Hoover on, then off, then on again, my residents screaming at each other in German over the roar. Next they were tiptoeing up the stairs, the whole herd of them, in studded army boots to knock on my door with a sponge, as my dead father would have said, fussing under their breath, afraid to wake me. Now you whisper? Now you are afraid to wake me? After waging an entire world war in my kitchen?

The aroma of Miss Berliner's eggless biscuits seeped through my floorboards. Toast was burning. The kettle was whistling. Take the bloody thing off the stove!

I hid my head under the covers. Didn't get up for two days.

———❦———

The strange boy never ate during the day. Every evening, the children set food for him in his special box. By morning, the box was licked clean.

They walked round the neighborhood calling "boy" into the bushes.

On the twenty-second of December, the coldest day of the year and Claire's birthday, a ghostlike whining grew out of the air from somewhere behind the right side of our house, behind the coal shed. At first I thought it was the wind, but within less than a second it was wailing, then bellowing into a scream, an insane, Olympian howl that obliterated everything from my mind but Claire and Billy. I darted for them in the darkness, colliding into the bedpost, not knowing, not feeling that I'd cracked my nose. And then it happened: the clash of the Titans, the planets and all the rocks in heaven colliding. It was a cosmic explosion, the end of the world.

Claire and Billy were in my arms, my refugees were clutched onto each other in the darkness, and the warning siren that had been drowned out by the missile was shrinking, whimpering now in terror. No light. Not in our home, not outside. Claire and Billy were attached to my nightdress. Ice cold. Shadows, gray and silent, were moving out of their houses as we and our refugees came out of ours, forming a shivering group in the center of the street like sheep.

We heard the air crackle like a cookout in the rain, heavy with the stench of burning. We saw heat rise in the darkness from the center of town, and smoke. Ghost fingers were growing out of the city skyline, lit from behind by fire—by an inferno reaching unashamed out of hell, searing heaven with its tongue—a heaven that was in any case closed. Hitler's bombs had fallen over Manchester.

A second time, the wailing grew to a crescendo out of a whining in the blackness; again the world came crashing down around us. I grabbed my children and ran.

None of us had been in our neighborhood shelter before. It was cold like a knife. The smell of cobwebs and mice attacked us as we got there— someone should have prepared, should have swept these steps ahead of time —though I knew the wireless had warned us so many times to do just that.

People were bumping up against us as we held onto the railing or turned to check that we wouldn't fall. Babies were crying. Billy and Claire were holding my hands now, their bodies shaking, so quiet I had to keep telling them not to worry, that we were safe. As though I knew. The shelter reeked of puke. It made me gag.

I'd forgotten to bring coats. My nose was pounding with pain. The taste of blood filled my mouth. My hand came away from my nightgown, sticky in the darkness.

We sat in that frigid, underground place. "Mummy," Billy asked, "are we going to die?"

Someone had thought to bring a match and a gaslight, so we saw that there were at least fifty of us down there. Some saint in curlers and a woolly dressing gown handed out blankets.

I held onto my children. *Please, God, let us live.*

We stayed there until morning, strangers nodding off on each other's shoulders, many—Claire and Billy among them—slipping from the benches onto the floor for more room. People were coughing. Some mumbled supplications under their breath. Babies wailed. As Claire turned nine, 270 war planes flew over us, dropping 272 tons of explosives and more than one thousand incendiary bombs.

I snuck back home the following day. Others did too. I told my group to stay put while I fetched clothes, blankets, and as many flasks as I could find of tea. Again we sat as 170 aircraft carriers dropped another 195 tons of high explosives and almost nine hundred "incendiaries" over Manchester; sat as our city crumbled into itself, as Billy asked if we were going to die.

We listened to the news in the deathly hush that came after, listened in silence as bodies of the murdered and the injured were pulled from beneath the rubble, from gaping craters and from wreckage that, two days earlier, had constituted our most prized buildings; so we remembered the numbers. Our cathedral, our Royal Exchange, our finest hotel, our Free Trade Hall—all of them blitzed to the lowest rungs of hell, along with the department stores we'd so loved. Nazi airwaves, we were told, announced to the world that our city had been wiped out.

Yet we were here, standing—neighbors and strangers—shaky, shivering, arms around each other in the most serious of circles, barking Rule Britannia into the darkness.

The boy in the jacket, whom the children of my house called the Little Lost Boy, never came after that. Every day, the children changed his food. The box was never touched.

The people in my home—the children—were so sad, so well behaved, so quiet. They never mentioned him.

I considered taking my children to the country where it was safe. But we had no relatives there. As for sending them off without me, even if I were prepared to part with them, imagine my Arthur coming home from the war to find that I'd given our children away.

So we stayed put in Hanover Gardens with our collection of odds-and-ends people: Little Annie and Myra, who talked only with their eyes; Miss Berliner, Frieda and Hanna Ungar, and Eva—all living with us until our English husbands decimated the Germans.

Our husbands, who couldn't kill a mosquito even if they banded together to do so, who'd back up and splay themselves against the kitchen wall when a cockroach surfaced, leaving us women to take down the Bug Off and spray God's living creature to kingdom come. Bug Off, I thought, now that's something we can rely on. It's Bug Off they should be shipping out to the frontline, not husbands.

Arthur had left me to my bunch of odds-and-ends people, to nights in my too-tidy bedroom—no rumpled shirt in the hamper, no wireless blaring the news so loud I had to burst a gut screaming at him because everyone in the neighborhood could hear it—and no one to hold onto in the dark. I was left to two children who refused to talk about their father, who didn't believe they had the right to complain.

Left to the half-empty bottle of gin my dad hadn't managed to finish before he died, to more bottles at Mat's corner store, and to cigarettes I'd stashed in my underwear drawer because I'd promised the father of my children I wouldn't smoke.

Disaster sat on my dresser, smoke blowing blue and curly from his nostrils, smiling, biding his time.

Ours was a semi-detached, brick house with an apron of green in the front for the neighbors to see how okay we all were, and a scraggy grass patch at the back for Eva to recover from her wheezing, her pallid complexion with its mysterious blotches, and her despair. That's where I smoked and podded peas when I wasn't at work, when the sun was out and the kids were at school.

Not that it was out that often; this was England, after all. It was there that the children played. There, their ragdolls faded in the sun and the rain while they mothered Claire's stray yellow cat.

Also out back was the coal shed, where Billy hid the second time the sirens went off, his dark honey hair and his freckled face black from the soot, his chubby little fingers with their dirty fingernails—he was always digging in the dirt—stuffed into his ears. I had run around the neighborhood screaming through the wind, like a she-devil, to the neighbors and the milk-woman who'd pulled her horse and cart up outside my house, because I couldn't find my son.

Our house had brown carpets and a sloped cupboard under the stairs where the broom and the mousetraps were kept, traps we never used because we couldn't bear the thought. Some months after Arthur left, I found Billy squatting on his knees in there, pulling my dad's broken clock apart with tweezers he'd taken from my bathroom drawer, myriad tiny metal parts around him on the floor. "I'm fixing it," mimicking his dad's matter-of-fact tone. "I'm putting time back the way it was before."

That was a laugh and a half.

My refugees didn't laugh, not the Ungar sisters or Miss Berliner or Annie or Myra.

A letter arrived postmarked. "The Netherlands."

"How can that be?" I asked the postman. "There's a war on."

"Beats me. Strange things are being sighted now that the Furies have been released."

"Furies?"

"You know, hags left over from the ancient Greeks, who never did no good for no one."

I could see why he wasn't recruited.

"My love," my letter said, "the sky is red with fire. People swarm the streets, mattresses, pots and crying babies piled on bicycles, donkeys, tractors, lawn mowers—anything that might carry them out of here, not knowing where to go. I miss you."

I filled my bucket with soap and water and went down to our basement. I stocked it with blankets, candles, biscuits, and water bottles so we wouldn't need the neighborhood shelter anymore. You'd think I was running a holiday camp.

My children were leaving food out twice a day now. Morning and evening, the four of them left food for the little lost boy. I didn't have the heart to stop them.

Myra

gain, Annie cried in the night, squeaking like a starved kitten into her pillow. I shook her, talked to her, pushed her body to the far side of our bed, but I couldn't wake her.

"Mama Heusen, I'm a good girl, Mama Heusen."

"Annie, it's me, Myra. Wake up."

"Mama Heusen, let me stay."

I couldn't wake her. I tried, as I always do, to talk to her of Mama, our real mama, but because I had to whisper, she couldn't hear what I was saying. I whispered as loudly as I could in Dutch so Claire and Billy wouldn't understand because I could feel them staring at us, as they do whenever Annie cries in the dark.

I wanted to be alone with Annie at night because I was her sister and it was my job to protect her now that we were strangers in a strange land. Before we left the convent, Mother Angelica had said that's what we'd be: strangers in a strange land.

"Annie, wake up. It's me, Myra." I raised my head and waved my left arm out of our blanket at the two sets of eyes opposite us, like a policeman at an accident shooing traffic away. The eyes wouldn't close.

I gave up, lay on my pillow again. Let her cry, I thought, because to tell the truth, in the year since we'd been in England, I'd grown accustomed to Annie's nightmares. I sank through the darkness into Holland; for the thousandth time, I went back and saw Mother Angelica waiting for Mama and me at the convent door. "Mrs. Feld, we'll take care of her," and a hundred times I pleaded and beat my hands against the window.

Sometimes Mama came back but couldn't get in through the convent door, so she stood, shut away from me in her blue woolen coat with its yellow star and her leather buttons locked, refusing to move or come nearer, which was how I knew she'd forgotten she was my mama. She couldn't hear me begging her to take me home, and in my dream I was never able to touch her.

Mother Angelica was there, hands clasped over her ring of keys, smelling even in my dream of mothballs. "God will take care of you. He'll bring you together again, you'll see." Mother Angelica was calm in my dream, quiet as the oak corridors of the convent.

Annie was still wailing. "I want to go with Annie," I whimpered, refusing to wake from my dream, and I saw little Annie swaddled as a baby and carried away in a car, smoke jetting out of the exhaust, and in my dream Mother Angelica changed into a lady with a sun-colored dress who laughed at me, and I knew it was Frau Heusen, that she was taking Annie home with her because Annie was fair-haired and a baby. She didn't take me. I was dark. I woke, as from all my nightmares, to Annie peeing a warm puddle on our English sheets.

I wanted to pray to sweet Mother of Jesus but felt I shouldn't do that in this place, not while Billy and Claire could see us from their side of the room and not while our sheets were unholy with pee. I knew Claire would tell me I didn't need to pray to sweet Mother of Jesus, she always did, so I stroked Annie's damp hair and arched my body away from the wet. I was sticky too, and shivering from the cold.

I felt for my rosary under the bedclothes and let Annie cry. *Enough. Stop. Please stop. How is it possible to cry so long?* I turned away from her, to the wall. *A faulty siren, that's what she is, on automatic, wailing after the bombs have dropped.*

We lay barred from the war by the blackened windows of this English house. The clock throbbed loudly in my head. I had no idea how close I was to the edge—never did—until I fell with a thud off the bed.

Dawn. Annie had stopped crying. I woke on the floor, Annie lying like a blond piglet in Claire's pink pajamas, sucking her thumb, her pillow and her sheet still wet.

Annie's pee-smell followed me across the room when I went to the toilet. Billy and Claire were quiet, didn't tease; didn't giggle or poke each other in the stomach, didn't fight. Billy didn't put on his scary black mask pretending he was the devil. Instead, he rolled his blanket from the floor and put it in the storage chest without Claire ratting on him ("ratting," Claire's term), "Mom! Billy's scaring Annie again," or Auntie Inda screeching, "Billy. Be nice! No one wants your silly games first thing in the morning," from the bottom of the stairs.

Claire gave Annie her Charlie Chaplin brooch to wear. "I don't care who he is and I don't want his ugly brooch," Annie said, when Billy tried to tell her about Charlie Chaplin. "I don't care who you are either. I don't want to live in your house. I want to go back to my mama and my papa."

Everyone said how good my English was, though there were still many words I didn't know. When Annie and I didn't understand, Claire stuck her shiny brown face and raisin eyes so close our noses touched. She shouted with her mouth as wide as a postbox. "Stupid," I said, right back into her face. "We're not deaf."

The house was cold. It was dark in the morning. Always. I lifted the blacked-out window. Outside was as gray as a coloring book with the outlines still blank. Claire thumped downstairs on her bum trying to get us to join her, getting angry. "Don't be so stiff, dummy. Bump down, like us." She stood at the bottom of the stairs waiting, her elbows bent outward, her hips pushed to one side, and her hands against her waist. "For God's sake," taking the Lord's name in vain. "It's not a funeral we're going to. It's breakfast!"

Billy rolled down the banister balancing his left arm and leg in the air like a circus clown, like the man back home with the monkey-organ, the holes in his red pants and his painted smile, who'd stood on our corner before the war, juggling rubber balls in the air. Until one day when he was not there, and the neighbors said was he was "taken" because he wouldn't wear his yellow star.

Billy talked too loudly in the mornings. "Jump! Jump down the bloody stairs!"

I didn't. I liked the smooth feel of the wood; it reminded me of the convent, so I stroked the banister and walked down. Claire said I behaved like a nun. They stopped telling us what to do after that, because they were in a sulk.

The warm milk smell of this English house greeted us from the kitchen, mingling with the stench of cigarettes ("stench," Claire's word) that was always there, though no one smoked.

It was Sunday, but no one was praying convent prayers. Instead, Auntie Inda greeted us on the mat between the stairs and the kitchen. We sat in a circle for such a small time it didn't seem worth the effort, repeating after her, "Thank you, living and all-present God, for having returned my soul to me," Billy scratching his behind as we prayed.

I wanted to ask Claire's mother what the living and all-present God does with our souls at night, but Claire was already up, pushing Annie and me like orphans, which we most definitely were not, toward the others.

Light floated on top of the air, in dust crystals in the middle of the room over the table. It perched on the sugar bowl, the only pretty thing in the room, and on the knife, causing its blade to glow. "Don't touch that," Auntie Inda said. "It's sharp. If you want bread, ask someone to cut it for you."

The light lay in patches, like house pets, on the floor. It sprinkled through the window in sun bubbles on the wall opposite the sink; then, when we weren't watching, it drew back outside, left us waiting for food in the English gloom.

"Move, why don't you. We don't have all day. Mom, make them sit down."

Claire's soul, I thought, still in its night storage, is bossing us around (expression from Billy).

Annie didn't move. She was looking at the sugar bowl. She was staring at the knife.

"It's a free world," Billy told Claire, already at the table, his back to me, shoveling porridge into his mouth. "They can stand all day and all night, if they want to," as if Annie and I were somewhere else. "Heck, if they want, they can stand there until the war ends, till Dad brings her parents home with him."

My heart jumped. It tingled in my eyeballs, on my skin, at the tips of my fingers, the soles of my feet. I yanked Billy's generous-hearted shoulders toward me until his chair almost toppled, blinding him with my arms across his face ("yanked," new word from Claire). "Yes. Your dad will bring them back."

Billy turned red as my mama's holiday borscht. He coughed and straightened his chair, buried his face in his porridge, and didn't speak another word.

Claire was staring at Annie and me, her head bent toward her shoulder, chewing the nail off her left finger.

"You are one strange person," and my heart shriveled back to real life. Frieda and Hanna Ungar were at the table too, watching, heavy-eyed and thick-jowled like antique spaniels. They were refugees like Annie and me, only they weren't waiting for their parents to come and get them. I should have felt sorry for them, but I didn't. They never smiled. They never talked to anyone but Auntie Inda, and they scared me.

I wanted to crawl into the dark space under the table with the cat. Instead, "Sit next to the Ungars," I whispered to Annie, but she wouldn't move. I've never known a person so small and so stubborn at the same time. Standing against Auntie Inda like a creeper plant, her tendril fingers ("tendril," Auntie Inda's word) intertwined with the straps of Auntie Inda's apron, clutching onto them.

No one noticed when Annie slipped the knife into her pocket, no one but me. I knew she hadn't recovered from her nightmare, and that she'd cry if I pulled her away, that she'd make a scene if I told on her. What would Auntie Inda do if I did tell? Would she send us away?

One thing I knew I wouldn't be able to bear, and that was more crying. Not that morning, not with Billy's blush and the Ungars' stares. Not with my shriveled-down heart.

"I won't sit next to the Ungars," Annie whispered. "They smell bad."

"So what? " I shoved her from behind. "Old people all smell bad."

Annie doesn't understand anything. At the convent, all the old nuns smelled.

They smelled of mothballs.

Auntie Inda's skin smelled like cheese. Even scrubbing the toilet and the tiles, or while carrying her mop and pail with those heavy gloves she wore for housework, even then sweat just beaded up, clean as crystal on her forehead.

Even then, it was as though she'd been washed with soap. Her head was curly like her red feather duster. She had pretty freckles over her nose, like Billy. She had them on her cinnamon-smelling hands too.

Auntie Inda was the prettiest woman I knew—except for Mama, of course. Her eyes were yellow with green speckles, like eggs from a hen. Mama's eyes were dark. There was a tiny gap between Auntie Inda's front teeth, like Billy. There was no gap between my mama's teeth. Her skin was brown like mine.

Eva held her arm out. "Come over to the heater, Annie."

"Move." I pushed Annie. She didn't budge (Billy's word.) "It's warm over here."

The day we'd arrived at Hanover Gardens, Eva was picking gooseberries in the garden, white like a lost swan. "It was easy for her to leave Germany," Claire had informed me, "because she's blond."

Each morning between the kitchen table and me, I saw the blond of Europe standing tall and mute on dazzling white ships. I saw them wave sheets across pale water as they glided away, silent as photographs, leaving the dark and unlovely in hiding places, smelling of fear. Claire listened when Auntie Inda talked with adults, so she knew about the war.

Eva never mumbled beneath her breath like Frieda and Hanna. When Annie didn't move, she went back to toasting and staring into the heater bars —no fuss.

Claire handed me a plate. "Eva used to have a baby boy." She was making her words very large with her mouth, thinking again I was deaf.

Claire and Billy held their bread up to the heater on the edge of a fork. I took my slice and stuck the fork in. It toasted gold with cruel burn marks where the fork had pierced it.

The wireless was playing war tunes. Claire put her hands on her waist again, "Those songs are soppy. If all our soldiers are doing over there is singing ballads and longing for England, who's left killing the bloody Nazis?"

Claire wouldn't let Annie be. "How'dyuspect Mom to work if you don't let go of her?"

Though anyone could see Annie wasn't "specting" anything.

"Concentrate on your own affairs," Auntie Inda snapped.

"You'd better put that knife back," I whispered from behind Claire's back, but Annie didn't budge.

To hell with her. I licked my finger and dotted my nose with the wet. I let Annie alone until my nose freckles dried, feeling pretty like Auntie Inda.

"Leave Annie to me," Auntie Inda told Claire again, though that was not what she should have been worrying about. "Look after your own affairs."

Auntie Inda wasn't our aunt. Papa and Mama didn't even know her. She wanted us to call her that so we'd feel belonged.

I didn't tell about Annie and the knife.

———∞◦❉◦∞———

One week after we arrived in England, Claire's friend, Sandra, walked into the house through the back door. From then on, she spent every day with Claire.

The first day, she presented Annie and me with chocolate. I use the word *presented* because she made such a spiel of it. Miss Berliner said English people also say "spiel." It means "big fuss."

"Here, it's old, but it's good," as though it were some rusty medallion stored in the attic since the last world war. "My mother said I should welcome you to England with it, though there'll be none left for us once this has gone."

Frieda translated. Sandra passed the chocolate to me before my hand was ready, so it fell on the floor.

"What is it?"

Claire glared at me.

"Don't you have chocolate in Holland?"

"They're faking so we'll feel sorry for them," Sandra said. "My ma said the best chocolate comes from Holland."

Frieda didn't have to translate that but she did, for good measure, as Claire likes to say.

"We had chocolate in Holland every day before the war," I told them, "with nuts, with nougat, with raisins, with candied ginger, with carrots."

"Carrots?"

"Eat it already," and Aunt Inda rolled her eyes at Frieda. "Go outside and play."

Annie refused to walk out the door. She does that sometimes.

"I don't want it," as though that conversation wasn't quite over and done with (English expression for "finished"). Annie had a huge problem with English life and the people in it.

"I used to eat chocolate at Mama Heusen's house." No one cared.

"It made my face lumpy."

She held my hand, dug her little feet into the rug so I couldn't move, though all I wanted was to get away from there, and glared at Sandra with her chin thrust forward and her face turning pink. The chocolate was gray. It lay clammy, like a dead toad, on my tongue.

"Welcome to England," as though Claire was singing a national anthem or launching the stinky bathtub of a ship that had brought us here (which no one in real life would ever launch) for its maiden voyage. Everyone in the room clapped. English people are weird (Billy's word).

———•••◦❖◦•••———

Trouble came in stages. First stage:
  "Has anyone seen my knife?"
  "Which knife?"
  "The sharp one with the bone handle."
  "No."
  "Sorry."
  "Haven't seen it."
  Auntie Inda had us climb into the cupboards and look.

———•••◦❖◦•••———

Sandra had oiled brown hair. Her eyes bulged like a frog's. Her top lip was heavier than her lower one, like a lid on pot. She let Annie and me play with them and Claire's ragdoll on the grass, as though she (Sandra) was the boss of us, as though we wanted to be there, as though Annie didn't beg me every single night under our blanket to escape back to the stinky boat that had brought us, which in any case had probably sunk by then.

It was Claire who wanted us to play. She and Sandra showed us where the cat slept, in a shed on a collection of old clothes. They let us play ball against the sunlit brick wall, and skip rope:

> Nebuchadnezzar, king of the Jews
> Bought his wife a pair of shoes.
> When the shoes began to wear
> Nebuchadnezzar began to swear.

I'd learned about olden times in Hebrew school, so I knew Nebuchadnezzar had burned the Jews' temple to the ground, but though I could imagine him doing much swearing in the process, I couldn't for the life of me (Claire's expression) remember a wife or shoes.

Annie skipped as Sandra and Claire chanted, but I was too clumsy (Sandra's word for me) to jump well.

"Nebuchadnezzar, king of..."

I watched the sun on the wall. I felt it on my shoulder. I smelled dust and wind. I sank through the sun patch to Holland and Mama closed away from me in her blue woolen coat with the— "Out. My turn," Sandra said.

"Give her another chance. She hasn't learned how to do it."

"She's still out and it's my turn. Besides, if Annie can do it, so can Myra."

"Well, she can't, so we're giving her another chance."

"Why do we have to play with them anyway? They spoil our fun."

"Because they're my sisters now. We have to."

"Billy's your brother. We don't play with him."

"That's because he's a boy, silly."

"I'm not silly, and I'm not going to play. So there!"

"You know what? You're jealous, that's what, because they stay with me in my house, and you don't."

"Yeah? I wouldn't live in your house if life depended on it, not with those ugly foreign people babbling about."

Sandra stomped off home. Didn't come back for a week. I was glad. I calculated I'd had two whole weeks in England without her.

—∘•◦❂◦•∘—

Three days later, sirens. This time, we used the shelter Auntie Inda had made under the house. It smelled like the public shelter of damp walls and mice, but Auntie Inda kept biscuits, water in milk cans, and blankets down there because of the cold.

110

"Just in case,"Miss Berliner said, when the blankets came out.

"In case of what?" Claire asked every time.

"In case."

Auntie Inda brought Uncle Arthur's shoes into the shelter. Two pairs. She shined shoes as we sat down there, handing them to us after she'd put polish on so we could brush the polish off, till we saw our faces in the leather while waiting for the bombs to fall. What kind of person does that? Three times she put the polish on and we rubbed the polish off—when her husband wasn't even in England to wear them.

At first, Auntie Inda didn't pay much attention to the missing knife. She felt sure it'd "turn up."

"Give it back," I whispered, but Annie tossed her head and ran away.

Peter was Billy's friend—tall, nose like a turnip, and giant hands. He and Billy were the only ones on Hanover Gardens who could climb the apple tree.

"You know?" Claire said Sunday morning when we'd lived in England for over a year and our English was as good as hers—almost; when no one was praying convent prayers as Mother Angelica had instructed me. "Don't forget," she'd said. How did they expect our parents to escape the war if we didn't pray?

"You know, if Billy and Peter can climb to the top of that tree, so can I."

"Yeah," said Sandra, "me too."

Annie and I went out to watch.

"You go first," Sandra said.

We watched Claire as she grappled her way to the top of the apple tree. Billy and Peter chanting, "Girls can't climb. Girls can't climb."

Claire's legs and arms hooked, tight and bony, against the dark bark of the tree. A row of tiny blood drops was popping up on the paleness of her skin, just beneath her knee. Her socks kept catching on the twigs; her mouth was pressed so tightly together, it lost its lips; and her face was squeezed until it looked like the fruit from the other tree, the one they called the crabapple.

Still, she didn't stop. She twisted and climbed and hoisted herself over the branches, her hair flipping red and glowing between the dusty leaves and the hazy sunlight. "There," her face pink and sparkling. "See?"

"Hurray!"

"You're not at the top yet. There's a branch above you."

"Wait, Billy, I—" Claire's foot missed. "Help!" Her voice collapsed high and scared, and everyone screamed as Claire flopped like her ragdoll thrown from the topmost branch to the grass below. Frieda and Hanna ran to the house, calling "Inda! Inda! Come," leaving Claire whimpering on the ground, her ankle limp like the leg of her very old stuffed dog, crooked and torn on the grass. Inda was working at the pharmacy.

Billy disappeared inside the coal shed. That's where he always went when he was scared. Sandra burst into bleating sounds and ran home. Peter stood over Claire as she lay on the grass, his head bent forward like a sleeping horse at a funeral.

Miss Berliner marched out of the kitchen door, her legs shooting out of her skirt like cannon balls into the air in front of her. She carried Claire in her plump arms from the tree, on the far side of the garden, to the living room couch, her arms as high as her legs, with us following behind, on silent parade.

Miss Berliner had a massive bosom and bumpy hips. She propped Claire on the cushions and poured what she thought was juice from a half-empty bottle above the refrigerator, which turned out to be sour wine from before Uncle Arthur left for the war. Claire coughed and spluttered through her pain, flushed in the face and glowing from sweat, like a hero.

—∞◦🔘◦∞—

Time passed. Auntie Inda's knife didn't appear. "I'm busy now," she warned, "but I'll get to it. I'll get to it in due time."

I searched through the kitchen calendar to see when "due time" was. It wasn't there.

—∞◦🔘◦∞—

Frieda and Hanna Ungar came and went together like the big-bellied twins in Billy's storybook, the ones with mushroom-shaped caps on their heads and turned-out feet like overgrown schoolboys: Tweedledum and Tweedledee, they were called. Everything they did, they did together. They fussed in German—Frieda and Hanna, not the big-bellied twins—hunched over the kitchen table drinking bitter black tea, Frieda in the fraying gray cardigan she never took off, Hanna with her brown hair, brown jacket, and men's leather shoes to match. They never took their eyes off Auntie Inda ("taking their eyes off," Claire's strange expression); rather, they sat with drooping jowls and heavy, spaniel eyelids.

"Sit, Inda. You work too hard."

Auntie Inda was too busy baking bread and curdling sour milk in sagging gauze bags over the sink when she was home, or sweeping, or paying bills, or scrubbing the outside front step even though it was certain to rain by nightfall. "You not do that," the Ungar sisters told her. "We do. We help." My English was much better than theirs. So was Annie's.

Everything they did went wrong. They jabbed at things too quickly. Frieda knocked Auntie Inda's groceries on the floor every time she brought them home. You'd think she'd learn. Hanna stepped on the cat as it sunned itself at the door. Frieda pushed the beautiful glass lamp over as she walked toward the bathroom. When Hanna moved to pick up the pieces, she knocked Claire and Billy's baby picture off the wall.

"I don't have time for your help," Auntie Inda told them, her voice low, flat and scary. "Please, do us all a great big favor—sit the hell down."

After that, they felt obliged to take their eyes off Auntie Inda, to put them back on the newspaper they kept open like a map, on the table, near their tea.

⸺∘∘❖∘∘⸺

Trouble came next on a Sunday morning, because Auntie Inda had free time. She rummaged through her kitchen drawers, moved the chairs, groped around behind the curtains. She got us, all of us—Annie too—to search behind the bureau and beneath the couch. I poked Annie in the ribs with my elbow.

"Ouch!"

"Give it back."

She rolled away from me beneath the table and went to the bathroom.

I waited until she came out, grabbed her by the wrist, pulled her up to our room, and closed the door.

"Where's the knife?"

"What knife?"

"Tell me where it is?"

"I don't know what you're talking about."

"Annie, if we don't slip that knife back into a drawer, Auntie Inda will send us away."

"Inda's not our aunt, and I want to be sent away."

"You'd rather live in an orphanage?"

"No. I want to go home."

"There's a war on!"

114

"Yes, and that's where I want to be."

There was no reasoning with her.

—⚬⊷◉⊶⚬—

Frieda and Hanna listened to the news all day, running to Auntie Inda to translate for them so they'd know if the Allies were beating the Nazis like they'd promised. Everyone knew both sides were going at it like sore-toothed tigers on a dead-end street.

"Not good you no speak German," Frieda said, as they went back to the wireless for more. For the life of me (Claire's favorite saying), I couldn't understand why they didn't give up on the news, which they couldn't understand in any case and which never told us anything good, and learn English.

Hanna slept on the couch. It was brown like the carpet, which matched her clothes. It was rounded with curved wood along the top. "Like a ship," Billy said one Saturday afternoon when everyone was home, "a warship on our living room floor."

"A warship," Auntie Indie echoed, singing the words to herself under her breath as she floated through the room in her yellow nightie, smelling of cigarette smoke though she insisted she never smoked, and of something stronger that I'd never smelled before. "A ship in the desert," she sang, "disaster standing by."

There were days like that, when Auntie Indie twirled around in a fog of her own, inventing songs, bursting into scary laughter, engaging in angry, whispered accusations against her husband's empty chair, then stamping her feet and turning it for punishment to face the wall, oblivious of everything around her. No one asked why she was like that. On those days, we acted as though she wasn't there because that's what we thought she wanted.

Billy leaned against the back of the couch, his feet dangling. "When I'm big, I'm going to join my dad. Together, we'll beat the crap out of those lousy Nazis."

Claire rolled her eyes—she was always doing that—and walked off to play with Sandra.

I stuffed my fingers in my mouth. *The war won't be over till Billy grows up? No! Annie and I—we can't! Can't wait! We need our papa and our mama! We need them now!*

The kitchen door slammed. Claire was back. In her most dramatic voice, she said, "Close your eyes. Dig between the cushion and the back, and you'll find treasure."

Then, "Make a wish."

I did. It was dark under the cushion. Again I tasted the dust of the cellar back home. I smelled toys Mama gave me so I wouldn't make a sound before we came out and I was banished to the convent.

I made my wish. Annie came in, scrambled between the cushions, found a tiny gold earring, which she pocketed, one of a pair that Auntie Indie had been looking for, for a long time. The other earring was still lost.

Trouble came on a Monday afternoon, after school. Auntie Inda was bringing the laundry in from the clothesline when she saw it: The wallpaper had a cut—a slash right along it, all the way from the back door to the kitchen.

"Who did this?"

No one knew.

"Get up to our room," I whispered to Annie. "Get up there now."

I closed the door behind us.

"What?"

"Give me the knife."

"What knife?"

"You know well enough what knife. The one we've all been looking for."

"I haven't been looking."

"You want to be like the poor little lost boy who had no food and no shelter at all, so he got killed in the blitz? Who had nowhere to hide when the bombs came so no one knows now if he's roaming round some strange streets starving for food—or dead?"

"How can he be roaming around if he got killed in the blitz?"

"You'd better hand the knife over, or I'll tell Auntie Inda."

"She's not our aunt, and you can tell if you want." I didn't tell.

———∘∘◦❋◦∘∘———

Frieda Ungar's hair was white, held in a bun so it looked like the metal sponges Miss Berliner and Auntie Inda used to scrub out pots. She talked more than Hanna. Her gray coat was so worn it had bare spots at the elbows.

Frieda and Hanna never opened their suitcases. They never changed their clothes. Their cases stood in a corner of the center room, permanently tied with string.

At the convent, we'd changed in and out of our clothes directly into our suitcases. We weren't permitted to undress there, even when we showered, for fear of what was underneath. "Because the body," the girls chanted in a chorus, the first time I asked, "is a dirty thing." I pointed out that it was dirty because we bathed only once a week and only in cold water with a nightgown over us so we couldn't see what to wash.

"That's not why the body is dirty," said Therese, the really skinny girl who slept on the cot next to mine. "It's dirty with sin."

———∘∘◦❋◦∘∘———

Trouble grew: a series of gashes, small but deep, on the living room wall. "What is this?" Auntie Inda asked, looking round at all of us. "Who did this?"

No one answered.

"Why would any of you do such a thing? Am I not good to you?"

No one answered. I wanted to cry.

———∘∘◦❋◦∘∘———

It was almost dark. Auntie Inda was herding us into the converted basement. It was a Sunday and we should have been praying. Frieda

117

and Hanna had grabbed their suitcases and were clomping ahead of us down the steps, banging into the walls, bumping into me, tripping over each other in their hurry as though the Nazis had already snatched them up, like Mitzy the cat, by what Claire called the "nape of their necks."

"Why don't you leave your cases upstairs? You don't need them in the shelter."

"Don't think we're safe, Myra, just because people are nice. We need to be prepared. All the time."

"Don't scare them, Frieda," Eva said.

"Who's scaring? I'm not scaring."

"You are," Billy said. "You scare us to hell n' back every time you open your mouth."

Annie thought hellnback was a country.

"Stop squabbling, the lot of you, why don't you," Auntie Inda snapped. "There's a war going on. It's right here and it's right now. What's more, one of you has just ripped my living room cushions— so keep your mouths shut and move into the bloody shelter!"

In the corner of the center room was a card table. On it was a picture of a girl with her hair flat over her eyes and no smile.

"Perhaps Claire could make a frame for your picture," Auntie Inda said. "Thank you," replied Frieda. "She's okay like this, against the mirror." One night I woke up thirsty, so I went downstairs for a glass of water. I heard Auntie Inda talking to Frieda.

"Are you upset with me? Did I do something wrong?"

"Of course not. Why would you think that?"

"Then why did you slash the hall wallpaper, the living room wall?" Frieda burst into tears. "I'm a good woman. I would never do such a thing. How could you accuse me of such a terrible crime?" I felt like a thief.

Sandra said if you look into a mirror too long a monster will pounce out and get you. I didn't know what "pounce" meant, so Claire acted it out in the dark, scaring the hell out of me (Billy's expression) though Mother Angelica had made it clear in the convent that we should never have let the hell in, in the first place.

In any case, I didn't believe Claire. I told Annie not to believe her either, though I tried not to look in the mirror in our room when I didn't have to. But the mirror stood on the bureau opposite our beds, so it was the last thing we saw before we fell asleep.

I couldn't sleep. When I did, I had bad dreams. I dreamed of my mama and papa, and of Auntie Inda's slashed walls.

I'd searched through every one of Annie's things but hadn't found the knife.

It must have been midnight. Our bedroom door was open and I saw Hanna walk out of the mirror, a nightdress down to her toes, her hair plastered in sticky clumps to her head. I lay riveted to the bed, not uttering a sound, wishing that Claire or Billy would wake up, praying that Annie wouldn't.

Hanna floated into our room. She stared at each of us, my heart ticking as loud as the clock, the clock ticking like thunder, much, much louder than it usually did. She didn't seem to see me. Tears were forming parallel lines down her cheeks. Her body was swaying side to side, back to front. I thought she'd fall. Then, without a word, she turned and walked back into the mirror, leaving the ticking clock sole guardian over us in our darkness.

Next morning, Hanna came to breakfast as usual, her brown sweater, her man's hair, her clumpy leather boots.

—◦◦❧◦◦—

It was Sunday and the sun was shining. "After breakfast," Auntie Inda told us, "we'll walk to the park." She went into the kitchen and there it was: a gash deep in the wooden surface of the table.

Auntie Inda called a meeting.

"Which of you did this?"

No answer.

She heaved a sigh. I wanted to cry. She took a cloth from the drawer, newly washed and folded. She ran it under the tap. Ever so tenderly, as we watched, she caressed the table with her damp dishcloth.

Annie and I will have to leave now, for real.

"My home is your safe haven. Damaging it is too small a thing to call the police, but it hurts my heart that one of you—any of you—would do this."

No one said a word.

Where will we go?

———∘∘❖∘∘———

There weren't many men in our neighborhood, only those, Claire said, too old to get killed. That's the way Claire said things. Uncle Arthur wasn't going to get killed. He was the one who'd sent us out of Holland, and Mother Angelica had said a special prayer for him.

August 1939, four weeks before England declared war, and many months before Germany attacked Holland, Uncle Arthur came into the convent with Annie clutched under his arm, his black sleeve draped over her shoulders making her hair glow almost white.

Annie's face was ashen with splotches around her eyes and mouth. I recognized her immediately, although she wasn't a baby any longer, but she wouldn't believe I was her sister. Stubbornly, she clung to this strange, dark man while he talked to Mother Angelica, his left hand resting on my head. I hardly had time to say good-bye.

Mother Angelica kissed me, smelling her usual mothbally smell, her chin bristly like a man's. "God will protect you. From now on, you must take care of your sister. It'll be hard for her—and Mary," as we were walking out the door, Mary being the name she'd given me when I first arrived at the convent, "when this is all over, you'll come back to us, won't you, my little friend?"

"I will."

I didn't pay attention to Uncle Arthur until we were saying good-bye to him on the boat. I was too busy thinking of what Mother Angelica had said. I knew God would never say no to Mother Angelica. No one would. I knew that if that's what Mother Angelica wanted, then that's what He'd do.

You'd think that would make me feel good, but the boat swarmed with people, all clutching onto their families and their bundles, so it was hard to remember what God would or would not do. Right then, He didn't seem to be doing much of anything.

Uncle Arthur had black hair and stubble over his face. He didn't talk much. In any case, the noise of the boat was so loud we could hardly hear what he said. He crouched down before he left so we'd hear him say that he was a friend of Papa and Mama's. "You must call me 'Uncle.' I know everything is scary now," which, by all accounts, was the understatement of the year. "But we're making things better for you. You'll see."

Babies were screaming. I knew they'd burst something if they didn't stop. Men were shuffling in corners, praying; others were with their wives and children eating bread and pickled cucumbers out of newspaper. The deck smelled of sour milk, of sewage, and vomit.

There were not enough bathrooms on the boat. Annie wanted to go when we arrived with Arthur, but the lines were long and she pretended she didn't until after he'd left and it was too late. I have so many memories of Annie, her pee and her vomit.

We were at the bottom of the boat, crammed with children of all ages, but Arthur had said it was healthier to stay on the top deck. A woman's brother died up there on the way over. They slid him off a board into the water wrapped in canvas.

They tried to make it seem better than it was by standing around and praying before they dumped him in. Some of the men, mostly the older ones, had their prayer shawls on as the captain made his speech. He said that the "deceased"—the word you use for a dead person when you don't want him to seem so dead—was "too good for this world," and that "God has released him from his misery." So there. God was doing something, after all.

The dead man's sister wouldn't stop wailing. Everyone else whimpered, though some were still munching on their pickles and herrings as tears ran into men's beards and women held their children to their stomachs so they wouldn't see the man being dropped into the sea. Annie vomited on her blanket.

Annie was like a smelly waterspout. When she wasn't crying, she was peeing; when she wasn't peeing, it was vomit.

The crossing took three days. When we arrived in Southampton, men and women in blue jackets came onto the boat. They told us we were no longer in harm's way, which made me wheeze, made me gulp for air like a fish snagged on a hook because we'd left Mama and Papa behind. Someone gave me a paper bag and told me to breath into it. That helped.

They gave us paper slips with numbers on them, making Annie think we were going to win something now that we were safe. "What do you think?" I snapped at her. "That they'll hand out balloons?"

We were told to wait until our numbers were called. Most of the people were taken to depots like the one we have here at Claire and Billy's school hall.

Annie and I were terrified that Mr. Garb's wife wouldn't come. She did, with Mr. Smith in his jeep. She was clean. Her hair was copper red. She had a green hat with a tiny feather that bounced as she moved her head and red lipstick that twinkled as though it were wet. "See?" Annie whispered, clutching onto my hand with her tiny, soft one. "We won them."

When I looked up, Mr. Garb's wife and Mr. Smith were running toward us, Mr. Garb's wife extending her arms like a scene out of a newsreel. When they reached us, the newsreel began to wind backward. They drew away by at least three steps, not wanting us, I could tell, to see how shut their mouths were against our smell.

"I'm your Auntie Inda." Mr. Garb's wife was forcing her closed mouth into a smile.

Little Annie pulled my arm, "I don't want them. Give them back." Before we left the dock, we had to go to a clinic where nurses in white coats cleaned us up.

"Did my husband send anything for me?" Inda asked.

"Yes," and I gave her the letter I'd saved for her. She didn't mind that it was crumpled. She read it in a corner while they shaved our hair and sprayed us against lice, like we were dogs in a country fair from before the bad times began; only there were no pink and blue ribbons, no dog biscuits, and we didn't come out looking pretty.

Mrs. Garb bent over the paper for a long time as she read. When she straightened up, her eyes were shining. I knew that Mama would like Inda and that Uncle Arthur would find Mama and Papa and bring them out.

I wanted to say something clever, but I started to hiccup. I wanted to say something polite, something that would make Inda like us, but every time I opened my mouth, parrots flew out.

———◦◦○○◦◦———

It was August, 1940. When I closed my eyes to remember Mama's face, I saw only Auntie Inda. Sometimes I saw Mother Angelica, sometimes a blend of Auntie Inda and Mother Angelica. I remembered the wide skirts Mama wore in summer and the mark that looked like a map near her ear. Sometimes, I'd catch a whiff of her, though I never saw her face. Papa had no face, just a pain in my head that made me want to cry.

In the middle of bringing in the groceries, I remembered Papa's laugh. I remembered sitting on his knee when he read us the stories we knew by heart, Annie on one knee, me on the other. We had to keep watch, make sure he didn't turn two pages over at once when he came to the bad parts to protect us from the pain.

I saw him standing in the doorway when we were taken away, his gray sweater, the quiver of his chin, the red in his eyes. I saw Papa when Annie stirred her tea. It was the way he had stirred his, with two fingers instead of one pressing against his thumb. Please, God, I prayed, let Uncle Arthur bring them out—and then I got the hiccups. Every time I remembered my papa and my mama, I opened my mouth and parrots flew out.

The only men we saw were Mr. Hughie, who spent most of his time at Mat Morgan's grocery store and who looked a hundred years old, and his son John, who was tall, whose left hand was missing. Then there was Mr. Smith, the plumber who lived up the street. He was short, with hair curled round the back of his head like a brush.

Mr. Smith had two curly fox-terrier dogs that looked like him. He rapped on our kitchen door every day. "Good morning, I've come to see how all of you are doing." I knew he really came to see Auntie Inda. "Arthur is the luckiest man in England," he said, trying to make her smile, and I prayed Uncle Arthur's luck would hold until the war ended.

Mr. Smith mended the kitchen window when it shattered in the blast. He checked the windows every time he came, making sure they were properly blacked out. He checked the shelter to make sure it was safe. I heard his voice chattering under the sink as he fixed the pipes, the soles of his feet (the gammy one longer than the other) and his bum in its blue pants sticking out of the cupboard.

It was cold in the shelter. I prayed to Sweet Mother of Jesus when we were down there, hoping she'd use her special relationship with her son for the Jews.

"Myra, luv, I'll teach you to pray the way we do." Auntie Inda was always going on at me about that.

Mother Angelica had called me Mary. She never told me I was Jewish. She taught me to pray the way they prayed in the convent. When the Germans came and they and the Dutch were pounding in the streets outside, Mother Angelica called us together in the chapel with the windows and the colored pictures of Jesus and the saints that loved us, and said, "If the Germans enter the convent, you have nothing to fear. God will look after us."

Mother Angelica looked at me as she said that. "We are all Catholics here, and God-fearing Catholics will be saved. Let us pray."

Panic snatched me by the throat. I wasn't Catholic. Mother Angelica knew I wasn't. But I watched her pray, her eyes holding steadily on mine, and I realized I had nothing to fear. When it came to the lying department, I thought, Mothers Superior had dispensation.

I thought about Mother Angelica and the children of the convent when we were in the shelter, and I prayed that Jesus would hurry up with his Second Coming.

Sometimes I prayed while I sat in the classroom because Annie and I were going to school now with Claire and Billy and their friends. The friends were okay, but I felt them whisper about me when they thought I was reading. That's when I closed my eyes and prayed for those I'd left behind.

All we ever did at the convent was pray: when we woke up, before and after the morning meal, before and after the main meal. Same thing in the evenings, we prayed. A lot of the girls were bored by so many prayers, but I knew that if I prayed, Mother Angelica would like me, that she'd persuade God to give me my family back.

—◦◦◦❧◦◦◦—

Eva walked us to school the first day because Auntie Inda was at work. Hospitals were so overcrowded that Auntie Inda had resigned from her pharmacy on Grant Street. She was working at City Memorial now, dispensing directly to the war-wounded and the dying.

It was foggy at first. There was no sky, only nothingness above. Soon, slivers of milky sun moved in and out of the grayness, dropping on and off the brick of the houses as we passed. The houses stood by the road with closed doors and curtained windows. Our feet clattered on the pavement, echoing the emptiness of the morning.

I tried to imagine families moving and talking inside those houses. I tried to imagine women, children, and grandparents clattering breakfast dishes, quarreling, eating, sleeping—dreaming even. I couldn't, though I knew there were living souls behind those doors.

People are like letters. Or books. They close too easily into silence. Annie was quiet too. I held her little fist in my hand, her fingers curled away from mine in a tight ball. "Are you scared?" Eva said we shouldn't be scared because we were the lucky ones. I pried Annie's fist open and found a gash across her palm, blood already dried and dirty.

"What have you done?"

"Don't tell. Don't say a word, or I won't go to school."

"What is it?" Eva asked.

"Nothing. It's a star I brought for good luck," Annie said straight out, in her regular voice.

And I didn't let on.

Finally, the clouds opened and the sun dropped quivering splotches of light on the grass. It moved along the houses, the sun that is, and a puppy ran out from one of the side streets, as though we were characters in one of Billy's storybooks, and loped alongside us, snapping at our heels as we walked.

Miss Walters was the headmistress.

"She's not much more than a child herself."

"Hey! You can play hopscotch with her between classes."—Eva who never opened her mouth at home, funny.

Miss Walters smiled and sent for a girl with frizzy brown hair and buckteeth to take Annie to her class. I got to go with Claire.

Miss Walters gathered all the classes together and addressed them in the lunchroom. "Assembly," Claire called it. I didn't understand everything, but I did understand, "Let us pray for our soldiers and let us pray for end of the war." We did. In silence, in that stuffy hall with its closed windows and its class schedules pinned to the walls, we prayed.

Mama and Papa breathed near me. I felt Mother Angelica and the children at the convent rustle near my shoulder, and I saw the other children reaching for their fathers and whimpering for them to come home. I closed my eyes. I prayed God to keep Uncle Arthur lucky. Suddenly, like a bandage being ripped off, the darkness flashed away. Light screamed in at the windows like an actual noise as I opened my eyes, and a shock of song filled the hall.

> All things bright and beautiful,
> All creatures, great and small,
> All things wide and wonderful,
> The Lord God made them all.

The voices were loud, too loud. The children around me were shouting at the top of their voices as though that would bring their fathers home. Their voices were quivering, pushing for something, arguing with God, angry at Him, frightened that for being angry they'd be punished even more.

They sang of rivers and mountains. Their voices rose and fell and soon everything sounded like an English storybook, like Billy's pink *Treasury of English Verse* with pictures of the Lake District on it. Still, they weren't singing about real people, about those that were neither bright nor beautiful, but smelly with fear.

In the middle of the night, Annie slashed her chest.

Everyone else was sleeping. I opened my eyes and there she was, whimpering, slumped on her bed over a ball of scarlet sheets, blood dripping on the floor.

I carried her to the bathroom, locked us in. I put her and the sheets into the tub. I filled the tub with water and an entire bottle of shampoo, and I propped her head up as she lay against the edge. I changed the bathwater five times before the red stains on the sheets turned to brown. I hid her cut with a facecloth.

I carried her back to bed. *She'll be okay*, I thought. I wiped the bath and the floor with the wet sheets, and I rinsed the sheets again. I crept downstairs like a thief, fetched the mop, cleaned the last smudge of blood from the bedroom floor, crept back down, washed the mop in the laundry sink, and checked the laundry cabinets for stains. With toilet paper, I wiped the laundry floor clean of even the tiniest spot, and I flushed the evidence away.

"What are you doing, Myra? Why are you up?" Auntie Inda was in the doorway.

"Annie had diarrhea. She soiled her sheets. I cleaned them."

"Poor thing. I'll go up and check on her."

"Better not wake her, Auntie Inda. She's just fallen asleep."

Doors opened upstairs.

"Has something happened?"

"What's the matter? Is anyone hurt?"

"What's going on?"

"Shh," Auntie Inda called upstairs. "Go back to sleep or you'll wake the children."

Annie was lying on her naked mattress, but she wasn't sleeping. I had to swab her cut and rinse out the bathroom sponge three more times before the blood stopped. For the first time, panic—scalding, ice-cold panic—surged through me. "Annie, do you want to kill yourself?"

I had no air. I gasped and gulped, but I couldn't breathe. I wheezed and heaved. I thought I was going to die.

Eventually, breath seeped back into my lungs, and I burst into tears. I couldn't stop crying, not when Annie threw her arms around my neck, not when she started to cry too, not even when she promised to stop.

I brought the First Aid box from the cabinet. I smeared Auntie Inda's antiseptic cream over her cut and bandaged it. I helped her with her pajamas. "Annie, I can't be in this world without you. Swear you'll never leave me."

———◦◦◦❮●❯◦◦◦———

It was September 1941, a bright, cold day with splashes of shadow on the asphalt. Almost three years in England. I was getting used to it, to England and to school. Annie was too. I could see she was getting better. She hadn't slashed anything in many months. She had friends. She was a runner now, the fastest in her class. Miss Walters said I spoke so well no one would know I wasn't English.

There was a girl named Sally in our class. She had greasy hair and her nose was pressed upward by some invisible hand against her face. Flakes of skin peeled off her cheeks and the backs of her hands. Her knees were bruised, and her fingernails were ringed in black, a badge of toughness that the others respected but from which they kept their distance. Claire said Sally's mother was serving time.

"Serving time? You mean, like Annie and me are doing here in England?"

"No, like being locked up in jail."

I didn't ask her why.

One bleak Tuesday during the break, Sally shouted to me from the other end of the schoolyard. "Hey, Jew! You over there! Why don't ye go back where ye came from, huh? Huh? My ole man says we've got troubles enough without no dirty Jews crowding up our country."

There was a hush in the playground. I didn't say anything. I wished the others would go on playing to cover up her words.

"Well? Well? Aren't ye goin'te stick up fer yerself, huh? Or are ye a scaredy-cat like all the rest of yer, hidin' behind us English? C'mon," she said, working herself into a frenzy. "C'mon, put yer spuds up and fight it out, why don't yer!"

She flew at me and punched me hard on my chin. My head jerked backward and I heard a crack as it hit the concrete wall behind me, the one with the ivy. Someone must have called the principal because before I knew that I'd fallen, Miss Walters was helping me up and guiding me through the grayness and the tiny blue stars that were dancing around my head and that made me feel I was at the fair with Papa and Mama before the war. She led me across the playground into her office.

She sat me in her stuffed armchair that was stained and kept for important people, not for cowards that had just fallen off a merry-go-round. I stared at the hole in Miss Walters's green carpet and saw Papa and Mama, the hopeless way they'd waved at me when they gave me up.

Miss Walters emptied the cup on the desk of its pencils and poured me some juice, talking to me all the while as though I were sick. My head was throbbing. I felt blood running down my neck, and I knew I was a coward for not hitting back.

My classmates were gaping at me from the doorway of Miss Walters's office as though I were a blowfish in a tank. Then, as though things weren't bad enough, Annie arrived, crying. She squeezed her tiny pink body through the gapers and threw her arms around me. Now I really felt bad. My fall had been nothing at all like Claire's, like the glorious way Claire had dropped from the apple tree.

The crowd at the doorway began backing up, making space. Sally was escorted into the principal's office. I stood up, swiveled around, untied little Annie's arms from my neck, and set her back into the softness of Miss Walters's chair. I walked between the math teacher and the superintendent until I was close enough to smell Sally. I took a step back. "My sister and I— we're not scaredy-cats," and mustering all the energy I'd ever possessed, I punched her full in the face.

The room spun round, and I blanked out on the floor.

Auntie Inda kept me home from school. I wanted to sleep, but she kept waking me up. When I went back, Sally wasn't there.

"They expelled her," Claire told me.

"What does expel mean?"

"It means she was sent away."

"Please, Miss Walters," I was standing in her doorway. "Please bring Sally back."

"Why?"

"Because she misses her mother and her father."

"No need to worry. We've sent her to a kind place."

That's what my mama and papa did to Annie and me. Expelled us. So what if it's a kind place.

There was a giant metal shed at the back of our school called the gym, though no one used it. Gym classes were held in the Assembly Room.

Friday afternoon, the first week of the winter term, my class let out early. I was waiting for Claire and Billy near the gate. The door to the gym building was slightly open. I'd never seen it open before. I walked over to look inside.

I had to wait at the entrance until my eyes adjusted to the half-light. The interior was enormous, like a train station with only two small windows on each side, darkened from the outside with sandbags. There must have been seventy people in there. No furniture.

Men were gathered in the corners, some in ones and twos, others in larger groups. Men and women were sitting or lying on mattresses spread out over the floor, sick, or too sad to get up. Several were squatting over bowls of food, in what seemed like family units. Near the entrance, a little boy was tossing dice. Others were calling numbers out and waiting to win. Most of the children were quiet and unmoving, like old people.

Blankets had been strung up around the mattresses, creating partitions— air, thick as porridge.

They were dirty, those people. Their hair was uncombed. Their clothes were crumpled, torn even. All talk stopped when they saw me. Some moved toward me, extending their arms. Those dirty people were refugees, from Europe, like me.

In less than a week, Auntie Inda was asking questions. "Myra, why aren't you eating? Are you sick?

"Don't take your breakfast upstairs, Myra. We'll get mice.

"Myra. Where's your coat? Did you leave it at school?

"What happened to your blanket? You can't sleep without a blanket.

You'll be cold.

"Myra! Where are your shoes?

"Myra, sweetness. What is the matter with you? You were always such a good girl!

"Is there something you should be telling me?" So I told Claire and Billy.

Two days passed, and Auntie Inda began pestering them.

"Billy, did you leave your jacket at school?

"Claire! Your clothes' drawer is empty! What have you done with your underwear?

"I boiled potatoes for supper. Where are they?

"Half the stew is gone.

"What do you mean you've already eaten? Where are your plates?" So we told Auntie Inda.

Auntie Inda sent Claire out the back door to fetch Sandra and her mother. Billy ran to get Peter and his granddad. Auntie Inda called all of us to a meeting round the slashed table.

"Myra," she said formally, "you are the leader of your little team. Please stand up and tell all of us what you've been doing."

When I told them, they cheered—Auntie Inda, Eva, Miss B, Hanna, and Frieda—even Sandra's mother. All of them burst into conversation, each giving off ideas, advice, warnings. Never, in all the time we'd been there, had there been so much chatter in that house.

It sounded good.

"Myra," said Auntie Inda, "if you want to help those people, go to the library, take them newspapers, take them books in German, read stories to the children."

"We wont to meet zem," Frieda whispered, pulling on my arm. "Will you take us to zee people in zat shed?"

Did I used to talk like that?

"Myra," Sandra asked. "I want to help too."

Peter's granddad shook my hand. "We are so proud of you," he said. Next day, all thirteen of us, carrying scarves and socks and soap and bags of food, paraded down the road to the school shed. Without a moment's hesitation, Frieda—defensive, frightened Frieda—strode from refugee to refugee, children too, with Hanna, who hardly even moved in our house, striding at her side. They shook everyone's hand. They asked each and every one of them their name.

"Pliss to mit you. My name is Hans." They were amazingly formal. "Pleased to meet you, I am Hanna. We are your faithful friends."

"Faithful Friends" became our name.

After that, we worked as a team. Billy and Peter and Claire went to the outdoor market scrounging around for leftover vegetables, bread, even meat. Miss Berliner cooked whatever they brought home. Sometimes the house smelled awful. Sandra and her mother walked from door to door of our neighborhood asking for anything they could spare.

I handled the deliveries.

I brought books from the library. The Ungar sisters formed two reading groups: one in the evenings for adults, the other in the mornings for the children. At the end of each week, Hanna had all the readers line up near the door and hand their books to her, *bittershen* and *dankeshen* repeating itself like the chugging of a train. Hanna handed the stacks to me.

I asked the librarian what she'd recommend for Germans. She came to the school shed with a book for each person, gifts from the city.

Neighbors came, turning up to see the refugees, bringing them preserves, pickles, soap, towels.

Peter's granddad brought his toolbox. He nailed hooks and shelves to the warehouse walls.

The headmistress paid a visit. Within a month, she'd organized English lessons in the shed.

Within six weeks, the mayor of Manchester arrived. He welcomed them to England and wished them well.

Articles appeared in the paper wanting to know why it had taken the mayor so long. What was he intending to do for those people? Why hadn't they been given beds, furniture, facilities?

The neighbors staged a demonstration, blocking the path so we couldn't even get to our classes.

A truck arrived with blankets and towels.

A man brought a crateful of dead chickens. We forwarded him to Hanover Gardens, and Mrs. B cooked them.

Claire and I arrived one morning to find everyone in a panic. Five masked men had appeared during the night. They'd robbed the refugees of their blankets and their shoes.

The Faithful Friends were written up in the *Manchester Gazette*. We were awarded a medal for our service to England—we being Annie and me, Claire and Billy, Peter and his granddad, Auntie Inda, Ms. B, the Ungar sisters, Sandra and her mom.

The shed had been eerily quiet the first time I'd entered. Now I couldn't hear my voice above the noise.

Noise, I decided, is a happy sound.

Auntie Inda put her arm round my shoulders. She kissed me. "Myrale, look what you've done."

I loved Auntie Inda with my whole heart.

February 1944. I was thirteen. The war got Sandra's father, got him in his plane. Shot him down as he was fighting to win the war. Sandra was sad now, didn't want to play, hardly ever talked, didn't even come over to our house. When Claire and I went to her, she held my hand and showed me pictures of her father. As we left, Sandra kissed me on the cheek. I would rather she were not so friendly and had her papa back.

For weeks at a time, the sky remained gray, threatening, heavy with rain, planes, and bombs.

Sunday again. We were sitting in the kitchen under a storm. Eleven in the morning and the sky was as dark as the tape on the windowpanes. Rain was tumbling over the house, smacking at the windows like enemy hands.

It was sticky in the kitchen. The stove was on and the windows were filming over the blackness outside with steam and tiny running tears of water. Mr. Smith was hammering under the sink, trying as always to fix the unfixable leak, whistling a marching tune as he worked. Billy and I were drinking milky tea, but bombs of thunder kept clapping out of the sky, and my tea kept slopping over wet and warm into my saucer as I lifted it.

It was four years to the day since Annie and I had arrived in England. The rain splashed outside. My tea splashed in my saucer, and I had to clench my knuckles tightly to stop tears from splashing into my cup. Soon, it seemed, everything would dissolve and merge into the black, frightening wetness beyond the kitchen door so that when Uncle Arthur came back, with my parents, to this island that everyone was so desperate to defend they'd find nothing but clothes in puddles on the kitchen floor.

The thunder was as cruel as the bombs of enemy planes, and a good deal closer. I wished I'd never left Holland; that I'd stayed with my parents in their hiding place.

"It's only thunder."

"I know."

Billy read my mind. "Let's go downstairs."

Auntie Inda sent us into the shelter with a tin of biscuits. We lit the wick in its smoky glass and looked at each other. I felt shy. I had never been shy with Billy before. I had never been alone with Billy before. I think he was uncomfortable too because he spent an awfully long time fussing with the storm candle and there didn't seem to be anything wrong with it. Finally, he stopped fiddling and faced me as though forcing himself to a dare.

"Myra. Do you like me?"

"Yes."

"I mean, do you like me more than you like Peter?"

"I don't know Peter."

"I know. But do you like me more?"

"What?"

"Because I think you're wonderful. I mean, I think you're heroic and noble...and pretty too." That's what he said. Those were the words he used.

"I like you too."

"If you want, I'll read with you from my *Treasury of English Verse* that you like so much so you'll be able to read like me."

I could still hear the rain. It was gurgling soft, splashy, and friendly above ground. We hardly heard the thunder.

We went down to the shelter almost every day after that and read from Billy's book.

> The small birds twitter,
> The lake doth glitter,
> The green field sleeps in the sun;
> The eldest and the youngest
> Are at work with the strongest,
> The cattle are grazing,
> Their heads never raising,
> They are forty feeding like one.

Billy got a prize at school when he recited that poem. "It's about peacetime," he announced to the assembly, "by William Wordsworth."

> There's joy in the mountains,
> There's life in the fountains,
> Small clouds are sailing,
> Blue sky prevailing;
> The rain is over and gone.

"That's the dumbest poem I've ever heard," Claire said. "Mountains and fountains and sailings prevailing don't exist anymore. They'll never exist again, and it's stupid to make everything rhyme like a song when there's a war on, which is nothing at all to rhyme about."

"You're right."

"What's more, it's silly to sit around reading poetry when people are fighting each other to death on the other side of the sea."

She was right.

Though Billy said I read the poem better than Claire. He said I was pretty. I didn't feel German when we read down in the shelter. Not even Dutch.

That night, I dreamt I was with Mama and Papa. They were smiling, and Mama was wearing the yellow dress with the gray collar and cuffs that she had when I was small. The room we were in was bright with sunshine. I think Annie was there too, in a basket. Nothing actually happened in my dream. My family sat near me and smiled the way people do in photographs, as though they have all the time in the world to be perched on those hard-backed chairs, and no need to go into the next room to study up on their English or send prayers of protection to their loved ones back home.

In school, as I pretended to be working on my math equations, I felt my dream wrapping around me like Auntie Inda's dressing gown.

———◦◦◦⚙◦◦◦———

It was ages since Annie last cut herself. I woke one morning to find her crouched by my bed, breathing in my face, staring at me. "What?"

"Get dressed. I have something for you."

She took me outside to her special flower patch. She dug around with her bare hands. There, buried in the earth, was Auntie Inda's knife.

Less than a week after Annie unearthed the knife, Auntie Inda emerged from her room with a declaration: "Up, up everyone. It's Sunday, sun's out, sky's blue, it's warm—we're going for a picnic!"

Annie said she had a sore throat. I said I'd stay home to look after her. Billy said he was too big for picnics and that he had homework to do. So the others went off without us.

We mixed Billy's paints to the exact shade of the wallpaper. We camouflaged the hallway so you couldn't see the gash. We rubbed shoe polish into the table—not perfect, but it would do, and we caulked up the holes on the living room wall.

That evening I whispered to Miss Berliner as she was peeling potatoes. I told her about Annie and the knife.

Nighttime, as we slept, Ms. B repaired Auntie Inda's cushions.

First thing next morning, we placed the knife back in its drawer.

Not a word was said about the transformation, but when we went upstairs at the end of that day, we found the note Auntie Inda had left on Annie's pillow. "Thank you. I knew you'd come through in the end."

There was another note on the dresser, from the Ungar sisters, in English: "You were not so good, but now you are good. We smile with you." And when Annie went to the bathroom, she found a card by the sink from Eva: "You make us proud."

Miss B. had made an extra pillow for Annie and me. It was pink with tassels, wrapped in brown paper on the chair.

And that, as the English like to say, was that.

Claire

"Ninety-eight, ninety-nine, one hundred. Ready or not, here I come!" I held my breath behind my mother's bedroom door so Peter wouldn't hear me as he clomped up the stairs. His footsteps stopped one foot away from me.

"Is that you?"

I didn't move. He pushed at the door.

"Found you!"

"You saw me hide. Come. Let's get the others."

"Wait, Claire. You have to kiss me."

"What!"

"You heard."

"Who said?"

"I said. That's the game."

I'd played hide-and-seek a hundred times, with Peter too, and I'd never kissed anyone. Nevertheless, I liked the idea of being kissed by a boy. I'd know what it was like and I'd be able to tell Sandra, so I didn't say anything. But as he pushed his face near mine, I smelled his skin, pimply and boyish and oniony, and I ran away from him into the hallway. "Billy! Myra! Annie! We're coming to get you!" Silly old Peter sulked the rest of the day.

Dad had been away for so long. Things were changing, and he didn't even know.

I wished the war would end.

My mom said Billy was too big to sleep with girls, so she made a bed up for him in the laundry room. He had a lamp and a chair and his bookshelf with the flap that opened into a desk.

And because he was by himself, he was allowed to sleep with Mitzy. Well, that wasn't fair. Mom hadn't wanted Billy to bring Mitzy into the house when he first found her. This is how that argument had gone:

"Please."

"Billy, I don't like cats."

She's so sweet. She's just a kitten."

"She'll grow into a cat. Cats aren't sweet."

"She won't. I promise she won't—she'll grow into a dog." *That* convinced her.

Now Mom was telling us that Billy needed Mitzy for company. For the life of me, I couldn't work out why.

Mitzy was soft. Her body stretched in and out as though someone was blowing air into her. When I passed Billy's room at night, the lamp shone through her ginger fur and she sat on the bed like a sun ball. I could hear her purring across the hallway. I wanted a cat too.

Four and a half years ago, when we heard Myra and Annie were coming, when Mom said they'd share my room, I dropped everything and ran to tell Sandra.

"We'll have midnight feasts and pillow fights. We'll tell each other ghost stories and dress up as princesses and imagine we're trapped in some fairy-tale castle and are waiting for our prince to come.

"We'll tell each other our innermost secrets and foretell the future out of a crystal ball. We'll transform our bedroom into our own secret temple and offer sacrifices to the gods." I stood just outside Sandra's room trying to catch my breath. She was sitting on her bed thumbing through a book.

"Why only one prince? Will I have to share?"

"What?"

"How can we have midnight feasts in a storybook castle when I don't even live in your house?"

—∞◦▶◀◦∞—

When Myra and Annie arrived, they were quiet and drab. Sandra said refugees were all like that, like Sandra's ragdoll when she was dropped alone in a dark room, gray and lifeless. Myra slept in Annie's bed because Annie cried so much in her sleep.

There were some really awful days when Annie refused to talk or move at all, when Myra hovered over her as though Billy and I intended to gobble them up live while brushing our teeth.

That got me so angry, even though I knew I should be nicer. I hated feeling that I needed to be a nicer person all the time. For the life of me, I couldn't work out why they were so awkward. I wanted to shake them into being normal, like us.

Sandra treated them like real people.

"Adam and Eve and Pinch-me-well went down to the river to bathe," she said to Myra, when Myra already knew some English. "Adam and Eve were drowned. Who do you think was saved?"

"I don't understand."

"I'll tell you again then, slowly. Adam and Eve and Pinch-me-well went down to the river to bathe. Adam and Eve were drowned. Who do you think was saved?"

"Pinch-me-vell?"

So Sandra pinched her well on her arm.

Myra didn't cry. She said nothing, not understanding what had happened.

"I like Annie best. She's more fun," and Sandra flounced back to her house.

"Give them time," my mother said.

I felt bad for Myra. Annie was the prettier one, with her honey-colored hair and her big brown eyes, so we were nicer to her. We told her she was Snow White. I played the stepmother because I was almost her stepsister already. I looked into the mirror in our room and said, "Mirror, mirror on the wall. Who is the fairest of them all?"

"Vat is 'fair'?"

"Fair means beautiful. It means good."

"I'm not goot. I'm playing with you while my mama and papa are in ze war."

Sandra made eerie, haunting sounds from behind the mirror until Annie ran away in terror, and I squealed with delight.

We had pinks growing in our back garden. Annie bunched them in her eager little hands. She liked them so much my mom gave her a patch of her own to grow them in. We showered her with flowers pretending she was the goddess of life, telling her, "Pinks are the riches of the earth." Sandra had read that expression in one of her mother's books. Annie burst into tears. She ground the pinks into the earth with her foot.

We lifted Annie into the baby pram and crowned her queen of the spring. She jumped out and ran to hide in the coal shed.

Myra was worse, too intense about flowers. She plucked them slowly as though she were taking a picture of them in her mind for some future use.

She showed us how to press the petals in books so they'd last forever. "That's dumb," Sandra said. "Flowers are not meant to last forever."

—∞◦◖◗◦∞—

Time passed. According to the news, the war would be over soon. When was soon?

Myra and Annie were going to our school, acting like normal kids, almost.

One day, Sally Smith beat Myra up. It was a big deal. Myra got badly hurt, but she punched Sally right back—full in the face. Billy and I were immensely proud of her for that.

"She's evil, Sally is," Billy said, as we walked up the long road home. "She's mean."

Hanover Gardens, our street was called, but it was not country-like with rose bushes, crocuses, and oak trees. Our gardens of Hanover were more like mats laid in front of the houses for the cats to pee on.

"Sally might be a mean bitch." My mom said I should never talk like Sandra. "But as it turns out, Myra gave as good as she got. Didn't she? As it turns out, she's not quite the goody-goody we thought she was now, is she? In fact, it appears that, of all the girls in our school, Myra is just about the perfect match for our Sally. So what do you think of your little goody-goody now?"

"She's nothing like Sally."

"She is too, Billy, you know she is."

"What is it with you?" I asked Sandra. "What do you have against her?"

"Well now, let me think." And Sandra hitched herself onto Mr. Hughie's wall and dangled her legs, so we all had to stop walking home. "When she's not being rough like Sally, she's being earnest, too earnest, way too darned earnest. No one can even talk to her. No middle way with her. I'll tell you one thing, though: One thing she never is for certain—and that's fun."

"Why is she no fun?"

"For one thing, because of the way she wants to borrow books from you all the time, Billy. Doesn't that get on your nerves?"

"She doesn't borrow books all the time," and I thought how lucky we were Billy wasn't in the debating society. Myra did borrow books from Billy, she spent a lot of time with him, and Sandra thought she was altogether soft over him.

"She's different, that's all. Foreign."

"She's different. She's weird, and you're sure friendly enough for the lot of us, aren't you? Just the little lovebirds, you are."

"Shut up."

"Shut up yourself."

Sandra got down from the wall after that and we walked on for a while with nobody saying anything and Billy kicking at trees so his shoes got scuffed up.

But Sandra wouldn't let go. "She doesn't even know how to play. Knows nothing, nothing at all."

"What's wrong with you people?" I said, and I hurled a rock across the road. "Nothing's fun anymore. All anyone does is hang around listening to horrid stuff on the wireless and jabbering away in German, or Dutch, or whatever language hits their fancy at that particular moment, worrying over Mom like ants over food spill as though they're about to carry her away on their shoulders piece by piece."

"Actually," Billy, talking suddenly like an adult, "it's not anyone you're talking about. It's Hanna and Frieda." And after another silence, "It's not Eva. It's definitely not Mom."

"Eva's not counted. She's pretty."

As though that made any sense at all. Sandra said such idiotic things sometimes. Then Sandra said, "She's strange, though, your Eva is. That's for sure. She spends all her time sitting on your back step, smoking. Never even talks."

I told Sandra what my mom had told me, that Eva had no family, that in her mind she was roaming around Europe searching for her dead little boy.

"Want to know what I think?" Three houses from home. "I think Mom is afraid of the lot of them, even Eva."

"Yeah," and Billy laughed... sort of. He was okay, was our William. Sandra's dad got killed. Shot down over Germany. Her house—my best friend's house, a house of mourning. Mirrors were shrouded over with sheets so they look like ghosts, the kind Sandra made jump out of our bedroom mirror.

I prayed my dad was not dead too.

Sandra and her mother sat on low benches near the floor. I couldn't think of a thing to say to my very best friend. I followed my mom up to them, and my face started to smile. I couldn't stop it. My stomach lurched. I thought I might well be sick. Then, just as Mr. Hughie and his son John stood up to pray, I started to laugh. Didn't want to, but I couldn't stop. I was so ashamed, so sorry, so sad.

Sandra held Myra's hand and said, "I was jealous of you because you were all together in Claire's house while my mom and I were here, alone. I knew I was sinning to be jealous of you."

———ooo◖◉◗ooo———

Myra seemed like a different person after she took that beating in school. More active. More normal. Sandra lost no time in telling us that, "Your Myra has had some sense knocked into her," but we knew she wasn't being mean. Not anymore.

It was Myra who discovered that the giant shed at the back of our school had people in it. It was she who got us all working for them. Refugee people, they were, like she and Anna.

Sandra slumped at our table one night, exhausted after having trudged round town all day collecting whatever people could spare. "Wow," she said. "Was I wrong about Myra. The whole town is talking about her. My mom calls her a force to be reckoned with. She's dead right!"

At first, I was terrified of the people in the shed, but after several times of bringing them stuff, I saw they were just like us, only sadder. Heck, we even wore the same clothes!

Dad would be proud.

———ooo◖◉◗ooo———

We had our chores. Billy took out the rubbish bins. Fridays, I sat on the kitchen floor surrounded by everyone's shoes and rubbed polish on them. The polish smelled spicy and exotic, and I daydreamed that I was a Hungarian princess forced by a wicked family to work, but that soon, if I rubbed hard and made the shoes sparkle, my prince would come.

I wasn't sure what the arrival of my prince would entail. The castle we'd live in was much more specific: white with gold chairs and baby blue bureaus full of treasure—my mom's garnet necklace that she never wore, *Oliver Twist*, my favorite book, and a stack of stationery to write home on. My castle had a hundred rooms, some for guns in case war broke out again (because it was peacetime in my castle and my mom said peace needs protecting, which was why Dad wasn't coming home). Some rooms were for parties that played my favorite music, some were to store my mom's sweet/sour meatballs and Miss Berliner's rhubarb pies, and others—for boys.

Each room of my castle was decorated in a different style. Multicolored streamers waved in the wind from the steeple. Across the road a field with cows and giant blotches of cow dung, the kind you shouldn't tread on because they're squelchy, stinky, and soft, buzzing with flies. There was a cowshed nearby with up-to-date machines for milking, butter-making, and chocolate-covered cheeses.

I'd seen cows, dung patches, and cowsheds like that when Dad was home and we'd driven into the country. I thought they were the perfect touch for my castle and my prince—first, because I missed my dad, and second, because I thought we'd go nuts if we didn't find anything to do out there in nowhere land.

⚬◦❖◦⚬

We should have been taking the train somewhere for our summer holiday, but we weren't because there was a war on. Instead, we were sitting on the grass shelling peas with Eva. Sparrows watched us on tiptoe, keeping their distance. The sun toasted our legs and arms. It shimmered on the concrete. We didn't talk much. We were waiting for something to start up again: sirens, planes. It was such a long time since the bombing we were getting used to the silence.

I was watching my mom scrub the back kitchen step white with pumice stone and water. She scrubbed on her hands and knees, kneeling on a rubber mat. Her body was slender, her green cotton dress clung to her hips, her sleeves were rolled up, and her hair fell in frizzy red curls around her face as she worked.

What was she thinking? I wondered if she'd look like that when Dad came home. I wondered why she hadn't given that job to Billy or me, why she did that job at all. Why does the back kitchen step need whitening once a week? Who sees it? Who cares? Sometimes it seemed she didn't know there was a war on. Why did she do that at all?

Mom said she hadn't heard from Dad. Why not?

We'd picked blackberries from the tree behind our street, and we were baking tarts with Mom. The kitchen door stood open because of the unusually hot summer and the smells of baking wafted out to us as we played with our leftover dough.

Billy made dough soldiers and baked them in the oven. He made them too thin, left them in too long. Most of them got burned.

It was quiet in our back garden. Mom said it was peaceful with the birds, the still silent air. She didn't look peaceful. I wondered if there were birds and blackberry bushes where the war was. Where were Myra and Annie's parents? Where was my dad? Where did the soldiers go to fight their war?

Why aren't they coming home?

—∞◦•◦∞—

Refugees don't sit on deck chairs. Sandra's mom sat on a deck chair every day when she came home from work; that is, when it was warm. She stretched her long, flat face out under the dappled sun of the shade tree and waited for her skin to blotch.

None of the people in our house sat on deck chairs, except Annie, who was not really counted because she was so small. She'd curl her wiry little body on the canvas for a split second before catapulting out like a rubber band and running off to hide.

Every now and then, for no reason, when she was rocking Mitzy and pretending she was her mother, or listening to Sandra and me, she'd wander off into a corner. Mom said sometimes Annie just needed to be alone. One gray Sunday, she exploded while we were playing cricket in front of the house. What's wrong with cricket?

"I von't play your silly English games!" And she threw the ball with all her might so that Billy had to run down the hill to fetch it. "I don't vant English games! I don't vant English," and tears gushed out and covered her little freckled face. She ran to the coal shed and squatted in a corner, digging at her eyes with her muddy fists so that her face was sooty and wet. She looked like the chimney sweep that used to come to our street before the war, so we laughed as she cried instead of being nice.

Refugees couldn't lean back on deck chairs, not while their families were "over there." So when it was really nice and when Mom wanted to get them out of the kitchen, Miss Berliner took Frieda, Hanna, and the wooden kitchen chairs onto the grass where they all sat stiffly, staring at their boots.

"Mom, why don't they ever talk about their families?"

"Because they're waiting."

I watched them holding their families silently in their minds, frightened to talk about them until the war was over and they saw what was left.

Will my dad come back? Sandra's dad hadn't. The little lost boy hadn't.

Nothing was the same as it once was. We didn't play games. Mitzy ran away. Mom said she ran off to find a mate, but it was raining. Some mornings, it was so foggy you couldn't see two inches in front of you.

The fog was so thick one Monday morning that we stayed home from school. Buses and cars were stranded in the middle of the streets and pedestrians couldn't see more than an inch in front of their faces. The Good Samaritan Home for the Blind sent its patients all over town tapping with their canes to find the seeing stranded and lead them home. Mitzy hated being out in the rain.

Was it raining where the war was?

——◦∘◦|◯|◦∘◦——

We heard Churchill announce over the wireless that war was over, and we ran out to the street. All the neighbors were there, even ninety-year-old Mr. Hughie and his overgrown son, John. Peter was there with his granddad, and Mr. Smith with his two black terriers. The terriers were leaping up and down, yapping, their ears and tails like little flags fluttering skyward, expecting a treat.

We ran to Crumpsal Square. Mr. Smith tied his dogs to a lamppost so they could see how an entire town of humans kiss and dance and cry. Mom danced with Mr. Smith and Mrs. Kaplan. Strangers put their arms around her, swaying and singing "The White Cliffs of Dover." Big John Hughie lifted Sandra's miniscule grandma in the air with his one good arm and twirled her around like a trophy on a pole. People came from nowhere popping tops off beer bottles. Beer foamed down men's chins staining their shirts. Women drank too and laughed and kissed like crazy.

John Hughie put his arm around Eva's shoulders and his voice sounded as though he'd swallowed mud. "Have some beer, love," he told her. "England is your home now." He leered at her. He rubbed his good hand flat against the front of her blouse. She stood still, never uttered a sound, didn't seem angry. Definitely wasn't pleased. Nothing.

All the while, a wireless was blasting talk and music over a loud speaker. Mom wrapped one arm around Billy and one around me and held us so close I thought we'd suffocate. "It's over, over," she said. *So why are you crying? Why are you making me get all choked up now that the bad times, when we should have been doing the crying, are over and we can go back to living the way we want?*

'Cause now for certain our dad will come home.

149

I'd never heard my mom cry. At that moment, I thought she'd never stop. Not that anyone cared. The entire world, it seemed, was shouting and dancing and crying. Some, as I said, were drinking and singing—and crying. Others were just crying. But my mother chose this particular moment to wrap herself around Billy, deep wrenching sounds like the braying of a donkey coming out of her.

Eva lifted Mom's head off Billy and sat with her on the curb among discarded toffee wrappers, beer bottles, and toilet paper that people had tried to transform into streamers. They rocked together like sisters with the crowd swirling around them.

It was then that I saw Myra and Annie, and the noise shut off. They were standing with Miss Berliner and the Ungar sisters, the lot of them stock-still in their boots and their darkest shades of gray. For the life of me, I couldn't figure out why refugees wore those clothes. They weren't dancing or singing or crying even. Just there, in the street, huddled in a group looking foreign and cold with pinched faces.

I walked toward them, though honestly at that moment I didn't even want to know them. "What's the matter with you? Can't you see the war is over?" I shouted way too loudly into their faces, as though they weren't just as aware as the rest of us of what was going on. "You should be happy now." I wanted to shake them.

"Your father will kom wit my papa und my mama," Myra said in her old voice. It was fear. Fear was making her talk that way.

Very formally Myra kissed me on the cheek as though she was appointing me mayor of Hanover Gardens.

"Thenk you, Annie und I will remember you always in our hearts." Next, Mom and Eva herded our group through the swaying, suddenly less coherent crowd, through the darkness and the now-frigid air with its looming shadows, its unfriendly turns, the drizzle that was beginning to fall, and the figures sprawled on the pavement or vomiting at street corners, to our kitchen.

She switched the heater on and made wine punch with cider and cinnamon sticks. "I've saved this for this moment," as she added purple liquid to the pot, and we watched, all of us, until it steamed.

My mom took her buckets and filled them with water. Miss Berliner got brushes and cloths and pieces of wire wool, and we set to work to remove the black tape from the windows.

But Billy switched the radio on to the middle of some celebration: Country music, of all things. Horns and strings, a fiddle that wailed and sobbed, that longed and laughed and danced all at the same time, dervishes coming out of our little brown box, swirling round us to the recorded pounding of some invisible dancers' feet. None of us, not even the Ungar sisters, could keep our bodies still.

"To heck with the brushes," and Mom pulled us from the kitchen. She set each person's arm on the shoulder of her partner and showed us how to point with our toes, how to flip our legs high into the air, to bob and bend, to throw our heads over our shoulders and twist our waists around. She taught us how to curtsy, to "match our hearts and movements to the plaintive sob of the fiddles, to the recorded sound of folk dancers and of breath."

Then the fiddles changed. Bagpipes—insane, primordial, at the same time arrogant and complaining—rushed like fire into our brains, erasing all possibility of thought. Mom handed open wine bottles to the adults, and before we knew it, we were thumping on the hard floor with our feet, twirling and leaping round our center room like none of us had ever moved before, Frieda kicking up her knees until we could see the garters of her stockings and the stunning white of her bloomers.

Again, the music changed. Little Annie draped herself over the back of the couch, relinquishing herself completely to the oboe's embrace. Her face was flushed, her eyes shiny as grapes. Myra danced by herself to the rhythm, reveling in the deep inner pull of the horn and the flight of the clarinet. Hannah swiveled round and round in a world of her own, her arms and face reaching for the heavens, till she swooned onto a chair with her blouse popped open.

By then, Mom was chugging directly from the bottle and falling over her own feet. We all laughed so much—we couldn't stand straight. Frieda was laughing! Frieda! Tears, pouring out of her eyes.

The music changed again. Horns. The trombone. Hanna recovered from her swoon. She wafted, yes, literally wafted round the room, from person to person, plastering each of us with whopping, wet, sloppy kisses.

I changed stations. Slow dance music seeped into the room, soothing us, calming our movements, our mood. For a moment, there was silence. Eva held her arms out to Billy. Ever so elegantly, she swung him around and taught him, "one two three, one two three," to waltz.

My mom seemed frightened of the calm. She flipped the radio dial again, searching, I thought, for noise. So much for Eva and Billy's tête-à-tête, because, voila: We had Russian music—wild again, loud, and ruthless. Silvery sounds that consumed us entirely. Mom rushed in, dragged us all back into a circle—and taught us the *kazatzka*.

That topped everything: We laughed so much Frieda peed in her pants, right there, on the rug.

Now that was a celebration.

Sparrows were chirping when we woke up—all of us on the lounge floor.

That day, Frieda and Hanna scraped the windows in the lounge. Miss Berliner and Eva took their room, which used to be Billy's. Myra, Annie, Billy, and I stripped our bedroom and the little laundry room where Billy slept. Billy helped Myra. If you ask me, Sandra was right: Billy was soft over Myra. When we were finished, we painted a giant purple heart on the lounge window for all the world to see, yellow roses dripping gobs of color down the glass.

The following morning, bold as some invited giant, as though there were no windows, the light stepped in through an open square in the wall of our room, doing what it had been denied for so long. We remained in our beds an hour at least, wide awake, before any of us spoke. Then, "This here," I told Myra and Eva, enjoying the drama, enjoying the pressure of the "p" sound against my lips, "This is peace. From this day on, everything will be full of peace. Peace is normal; no sirens, no blackened windows."

And Myra said, "For us it is not normal to be widout our papa und our mama."

An entire war had been fought and won and I hadn't yet learned how to say what was needed. Beneath my covers, I prayed for Myra and her parents.

Maybe they'll come home, all of them together, today.

——∞◦❀◦∞——

I was lying on my bed again two and a half months later. It was a long, late summer evening and I was fascinated by the chortlings of frogs and crickets outside our window. Had they been there during the war? That summer, the sky never seemed to grow dark. I heard John Hughie mowing his lawn. I smelled the sweetness of cut grass. Mom and Miss Berliner were outside on their deck chairs. Yes, deck chairs. Their voices tinkled like stacking china on the air.

It's been two months since the war ended. My dad isn't home.

——∞◦❀◦∞——

Hanna and Frieda had moved to a tiny apartment above a fish 'n' chips place on Chester Street where they took in clothes and sewed for people. Miss Berliner took me to see them one Sunday afternoon. We walked for a full fifty minutes past the bombed-out city center, through neighborhoods I'd never seen before, until we arrived at a cement block with tiny windows and no balconies on a street bare of vegetation—not a tree or bush in sight. Frieda and Hanna's apartment was on the ground floor, which was good, Miss Berliner said, because that made them easier to find. A sign on their front door read,

> The Ungar Inn. Five shillings per night.
> Shower–6p.
> Towel–On the house.

153

There was a bed with a pillow and a striped blanket folded on it in the bedroom, and a green striped couch in the living room with a blanket and a cushion on that too. "Gifts from friends," Hanna said, though in all the time they'd lived in our house, I'd never seen a friend. There was a gas burner, a card table with a floral tablecloth, and a wireless perched on top that Mr. Smith had given them, ready to tell the news every fifteen minutes.

The afternoon hovered over the sink. A breeze was blowing their curtain gently, at the window, flat and colorless as the end of a sigh. They had geraniums growing in pots on the sill between the picture I remembered of the unsmiling girl with the straight-cut hair and bangs, and a heart-shaped cushion full of pins. The cushion was shiny red and really ugly. It was mounted, for show, on a specially crafted wooden platform, a gift from a customer, Frieda told us, because she'd taken in his pants. No charge.

Hanna and Frieda drank their tea with Miss Berliner and me out of washed-out candle glasses, the kind used for memorials or deaths. The tea tasted of fish 'n' chips because of the smell from the shop below, making me realize how famished I was, and how I shouldn't let on. The women drank theirs black and strong as always, only now they each had a sugar cube to sweeten it.

"A man needed a place to stay," Hanna told us. "He slept on the couch for two nights and paid us in cubes of sugar." Sipping their tea in the grayish yellow light of the late afternoon, the sisters' fidgeting, the chattering I'd always taken as an integral part of their personalities, slowed to a stop. They were sucking something in with that sugared tea that only they could see.

I left them to their thoughts and wandered round the one and a half rooms. No suitcase. Not even string. As though they had sat at that card table in their Ungar Inn their whole lives.

We started our long walk home.

"Why don't they ever talk about the girl in the picture?"

"She was shot in the street by the SS, and it hurts too much. She was Frieda's only child."

When? Was it before they left Europe or while they were with us? I wanted to ask, but that door seemed to have closed.

We walked in silence through the shopping district and up the long hill past the library. When we reached the school, Miss Berliner started to talk again. She told me she'd worked as a cook before the war, which was why she helped my mom so much in the kitchen. I looked at her gnarled body. Her shoulders were like cushions and her legs were bowed, bulging with veins, the leather on her shoes stretched by her toes. The knuckles on her hands were bony; tiny hairs and purple veins had taken up living quarters on her cheeks.

She talked to me as though I were an adult. She must be lonely in our house, I thought, now that the others have left.

"I was in love once with a man called Friedrich." We continued walking for another five minutes, neither of us talking. I wasn't sure if I was allowed to be curious about Friedrich. I mean, how was I meant to know what I could or could not ask?

"What was he like?"

"Aah! He was a man!" And Miss Berliner walked on as though she'd answered me.

Ten minutes further. We were almost home. She stopped, placed her hand on my shoulder. "He was calm, always," she said. "Skin? Like linen. Hair? Satin."

Miss Berliner kissed the tips of her fingers, as though she could taste him.

"And a voice? Such loving he had in his voice. We had a cafe in the hills with a room on top. He made soup from mushrooms he picked in the forest, and he sang to the customers as they ate. Today, we would have been married seven years."

Miss Berliner was so solid. I looked at her body and tried to imagine her seven years younger and in love with Friedrich. I tried and I failed. I felt mean. She talked about Hitler all the time, more now that the war was over.

"Hitler is living in the mountains," she said. Hitlers never die, making me want to run, hide, bury myself under the house, panic

155

about what would happen to mom and the others if I did—as we finally turned into the street that led into ours.

Did Hitler kill my dad?

People were coming back. One windy afternoon, a man delivering milk from a horse-drawn cart appeared. The horse was too large for the cart. It neighed and reared when the man removed the milk can from the wagon, or when he tried to tie the food sack round its neck. The man's hand shook. He spilled the milk as he poured it into the neighbors' containers. Anyone could see he was scared of his horse.

A peddler rolled up our street with a barrow of brushes, brooms, and ladies' lipsticks. He stayed for a bit after the women had finished their purchases, joking with the kids who were clustered around, asking him if he had games for sale, wanting to know if he'd fought in the war and if he'd killed anyone. He was mean-looking, with a scar down the side of his face.

"Well, you're a pretty one. What's your name, luv?"

"What's it to you?" My mom hated when I was rude. "Feisty, is it? Tell ole Sam your name, luvy." I didn't answer.

He lowered his voice to a growl. "If yer don't tell me yer name, I'll come back one dark night...an get yer."

I walked up the road away from him, forcing my legs to move slowly so he wouldn't think I was afraid. I walked right past my house so he wouldn't see where I lived.

What if there are more Hitlers? Many more? Living in Europe? In England?

After that, I kept my bedroom window closed. I tried to keep myself from thinking of the man's pasty skin and his moustache. Maybe he was the real Hitler, the bad one. Maybe Miss Berliner was right, that Hitlers never die.

Now that the war was over, I had dreams. I dreamt that my father was coming down the mountains. He was running down toward Mom and Billy and me. I could tell he was happy to be coming home because he was smiling. He had a flute and was playing music. Crowds of children grew out of the shrubbery on the mountain and ran down around him as though he was the Pied Piper, only he was wearing an army uniform. Then my dream changed. As the children came near, I saw that they were wearing brown shirts and armbands. They were stomping their feet in thick, heavy boots and waving their fists in a menacing way, and my father was suddenly not my father but Hitler, and Hitler was my father and his flute was a gun and was pointed at me.

I screamed and woke up. Myra got up and hugged me, kneeling next to my bed. She brought me back into the morning and our brown room with the window wide open because the war was over. I hadn't told her about the peddler with the wagon who might be Hitler, and who might come back to get me if he meant what he'd said. The scary outdoor air was spilling, unchecked, into my bedroom. "My dad. It was my dad."

"I dream too," Myra is so sad, "That's how I stay close to Papa und Mama."

I looked at my friend's serious face. "Poor Myra, it must be so hard for you and Annie not knowing where your parents are."

"You don't know where your papa is either, "and I froze. *Please, God, don't let them be dead,* and Myra heard me, "I know your father is okay. That he will bring my papa und my mama out."

I hugged her.

———◦◦◦|◦|◦◦◦———

Myra and Annie's papa came back. I was glad for them, they deserved it. His name was Mr. Feld. My dad found him in a displaced persons camp, Mom said, and sent him to us. My dad found Sandra's grandfather too, her murdered dad's father. He arrived more than a month before Mr. Feld. Sandra's mom was so excited when she got the letter saying he was arriving; she couldn't stop jumping up and down, dancing round our kitchen and hugging my mom. She talked a lot too—nonstop, in fact.

She painted their spare room for him in two shades of blue, and she had Mr. Smith build extra shelves in the wardrobe. She bought him a giant glossy picture book of the England countryside to keep next to his bed, and she bought pills on the street from a vendor with a cart. I prayed it wasn't my vendor, the one that might be Hitler, who might still come back one night to get me.

The vendor told Sandra's mom that his pills were new on the market, that they were made from Chinese pig skins, monkey livers, and pearls from the bottom of the ocean, and that they were guaranteed to heal all her father-in-law's pains and make him twenty years younger. She said she'd have bought a bottle for herself too but they were expensive. She said she'd use her father-in-law's when he recovered from his war wounds, but she wouldn't wait till he looked too young, as that wouldn't be proper for him at his stage in life. She and Sandra took the train to the docks to bring him home.

Her excitement didn't last. Three weeks in and she was already telling Mom how irritating it was to have her father-in-law in the house. "He's cranky. He snores so loudly I can hear him through the wall. I can't sleep at night because of the noise he makes. His teeth are rotting in his mouth and he doesn't smell that good. I've forbidden him to eat garlic, or to fry onions—he loves frying onions. Believe me, Inda, the last thing I need, at my time of life, is to look after an old man who is half deaf and, in any case, can't understand a word I say."

"What will you do? Send him away?"

"Now, Inda, why would I do a thing like that?"

"Because you don't want him."

"Of course I want him. He's alive. We're family. He's my Robert's father."

We walked home.

"Where's *our* dad?"

"I don't know."

"Why hasn't he come? He's allowed to be home now. Doesn't he miss us?"

"He's no doubt roaming round Europe looking for people to save."

"Aren't you angry that he doesn't want to be with us?"

"Everyone needs a hero." My mom was chewing on her lip as she said that. "Your dad is mine. Besides, I know he wants to be with us."

—∞◦◦🞙◦◦∞—

Mr. Smith took Mom to bring Mr. Feld home in the old green jeep. He'd spent six weeks in a hospital before coming to us. He told Mom and Mr. Smith that he'd hidden on a farm in Holland for the duration of the war. The farmer and he ran out of food long before the war ended, so he and the "righteous Gentile"—that's what he called the man who had hidden him— gulped raw flour from sacks to stay alive. They washed it down with rainwater.

"Your mama is gone," Mr. Smith told Annie and Myra, holding them firmly by their hands. Annie looked at him as if she'd known all along, her lips pinched and angry. "I don't remember my mama. I can't remember her face when I close my eyes." She drew her hand away from Mr. Smith. She refused to cry.

Myra turned to face my mother. "You promised me." I could hear the scream she was holding from us behind her words. "You promised. You said your Arthur was the luckiest man in England."

She went upstairs. I found her kneeling by the bed. It was a long time since I'd seen her rosary. Billy was standing near her door, frightened to talk.

"It's not enough to be nice," she said. I sat on the edge of her bed. "We wanted too moch. One of them had to lose..."

Please, God, let my dad not be dead too.

When I saw Myra and Annie's father, I was sure he had no bones in his body, that he was held together by gelatin. Two gray hairs lay flat on his head. That's all. The rest was bald. His voice was not much more than a whisper. He had the saddest eyes, gray liked Myra's, only empty, empty and dry.

They weren't allowed to remain in England, Mr. Smith told us, because of what Mom called the "quota."

"I don't want to stay," Mr. Feld said. "I want to take my girls as far avay as I can and start again."

After a few weeks, they left for Australia, and we went to see them off at the docks. Annie clung to the ragdoll Sandra and I had given her. "Promise to come when your Arthur comes back. Please, please promise." And we did. Myra kept her arms around my mom, her face a bleached-out brown against mom's shoulder. She didn't shed a tear. "Whatever I do in my life, you must know, I will always love you."

Myra and Annie gave Billy and me a gift. It was the first verse of Auld Lang Syne printed in pressed daisy and dandelion petals plucked from our garden. Billy and I gave them our *Treasury of English Verse* from school, which Billy used to read with Myra. Mom gave Myra her own prayer book and my dead grandma's candlesticks from the back of the kitchen cupboard.

The week after that, Eva left too, back to Europe, which worried my mom no end, to work in refugee camps. John Hughie was waiting for her at the train station when we got there. He brought her daisies, the big kind, tied together with straw. He stood on the platform, broad-backed and hopeless with tears in his eyes. When she boarded, he handed her something wrapped in a cloth.

"Wow," Billy's eyes almost shot out of his face, "A pistol—a real, live pistol."

"Take it," John Hughie was handing the gun to Eva. In case..."

Big John Hughie must have had another pistol because the very next day, he shot himself. Mom made us all dress up in black and go to his funeral.

I couldn't sleep. I lay awake at night, biting my fingernails, begging God not to let my dad be dead.

Miss Berliner was staying on with us, until she found a job as a cook.

———∘∘🔯∘∘———

"Billy's father is coming home."

"Why do you keep telling people that Billy's father is coming home?" as though my mom couldn't understand, "He's your dad too."

"I don't know what he looks like."

"He's handsome, and he's your dad, and he loves you, and you love him!"

"All right. You don't have to shout."

It was nighttime. We were in bed. Mom called us from downstairs, her voice high as glass, light like a young girl's.

He was standing at the foot of the stairs. Dark. Gray shadows under his eyes and beneath his cheekbones, worn-looking and wild. He wore a soldier's uniform and a beard that was blacker than black. Bushy. I was sure it wasn't real. I swear I had never seen that man in my life.

His bag bulged from his left hand, and his right arm hung heavily around Mom's shoulders as though he owned her. His eyes glowed with a dull black light, and his teeth shone white over his beard.

"Leave her alone."

"Claire, luv, it's your dad. Come down. Say hello."

The man's smile faded. He was looking at Billy and his eyes were gentle and heavy now because Billy was doing the strangest thing. Riveted to the spot, he was, on the top of our stairs, stiff and unmoving like a cardboard cutout. His eyes were bulging from his round little face. His face had no color. He didn't blink, didn't move a muscle.

The man eased his bag to the floor, and that's when I saw it: his limp. The entire right side of his body heaved over when he took a step. A gammy leg, he had, like Mr. Smith from up the road—worse than Mr. Smith's, far, far worse. Carefully, like an injured lion in nature films, the man lurched his body up the stairs to Billy, two steps at time, never taking his eyes off him.

He lifted Billy onto his crooked shoulder, but Billy's body wouldn't soften. It stuck out stiff in the air away from his father as if it were starched. It didn't hear his father. Didn't even hear our mom, though Mom was fussing and crooning into his ear.

"Billy, luv, it's your dad. Your dad's come home."

The man held Billy tight and quiet, murmuring in a low voice down the back of his neck until something in him snapped and he fell down limp, lay in the man's arms like the wet gauze Mom hung over the sink to make cheese. They brought Billy downstairs and covered him with the checkered blanket that Miss Berliner had knitted from the wool of our old jerseys. He was all right after that.

The man made me sit on his knee, though I was obviously too big, and he kissed me and told me I was beautiful and that he'd forgotten how curly my hair was.

He smelled of trains and smoke and leather and dry grass. His right hand trembled, I didn't know why, and his khaki jacket enveloped me scratchy and warm against my skin. I didn't cry.

Next day, we sat on Mom's big bed and watched as she made Dad shave off his beard. He made faces and pretended he was miserable because she was the boss and she wouldn't let him keep it. His body was still crooked.

Billy jumped up and down. "Don't shave it off. It looks good." Our father winked at us through the mirror in the wardrobe door.

Mom brought steaming hot soup into the bedroom. She never let us eat in the bedroom. She spooned the liquid directly into our father's mouth, saying, "Here, luv, drink. It will make you strong again."

Then she sat back in her wide wicker chair wearing the apple-green dress with the tiny flowers and the very full skirt that Aunt Sue had sent from America, and smiled.

You'd think he'd had never been away at all.

———∞•◗●◖•∞———

There was a fireplace with a metal guard in our school lunchroom. We weren't allowed to touch the guard because if it fell, the sparks or the hot coals could hit us.

Little Annie was sitting on the floor, playing. I went up to her. She smiled at me. I lifted her up above my head, my arms waving in the air like snakes, and Annie looked down at me again and smiled. I smiled back. I threw her over the fireguard into the flames, and the flames surged up and roared huge and orange, and I screamed and screamed and stumbled up and out into my parents' darkened bedroom, and cried and mumbled. My dad got up and folded his arms around me. His pajama folds and his warm smell hushed me. Slowly, he took me back to my room. "It was just a dream," he said. "Say your prayers and it'll go away."

I developed a trick to make me sleep. If I forgot it and slept on my right side, I had bad dreams. I dreamt of fire, of Nazis, and of Miss Berliner's mountains. But if I slept on my left side toward the open door, I'd dream that I was a princess in a white tower with blue and gold turrets, and that my prince would come.

I always woke up before the happy-ever-after you read about in books.

———∞•◗●◖•∞———

Myra was walking to school with Sandra and me. I ran on ahead and Sandra followed. We turned and laughed at Myra, though I felt bad doing that because Myra looked so pale. Myra slowly, ever so slowly, turned and walked away from us down the middle of the street. Her school bag dragged on the ground and blood trickled out of it.

I woke and listened to the stillness of my room until it started to creak and breathe and I thought of Myra.

163

I felt her near me in the darkness and I heard her voice. I thought of her mama and of Sandra's father, and of those silent people in Germany whom Miss Berliner and the Ungar sisters kept in picture frames and whom they were trying, Mom said, to locate. I felt a pressure on my ears. Silent voices were pressing near me in the moving air of my room. I saw a myriad nameless faces that I had never known. I heard my parents talking of war, of the dead and the living, and of the awful things that had happened to those who lingered in between.

Downstairs at night my parents had meetings. Words I didn't understand repeated themselves in the still darkness of my room: Communists. Fascists. Nazis. Threat. I dreamed. I dreamed that Nazis and communists were coming together down the mountains, stealthily and slowly while my parents and their friends nibbled nuts and raisins in the room below.

They rumbled as they surged toward us. They threw words at us. They were the communists and the fascists. They were my parents and Billy and me. I didn't know what I was or what they were or whether we were the same, or separated by those words that had a power behind them as awful as the war. My greatest fear was that I'd be separated from my family by one of those words that rose up at me out of the darkness.

——◦◦◦◦◦◦——

One rain-drenched morning, we received a letter from Australia. Mr. Feld was working and living, it began, on a farm with his Annie. "Myra left us for a while, back to the convent that had taken her as a child. She begged me to let her go. I mourned my wife, and I missed my eldest daughter, though I thanked God she was alive and I prayed daily that she'd find comfort.

"Friday last, nine in the morning," the letter told us, "Myra walked in through our kitchen door as we were finishing breakfast, unpacked the few clothes she owned and the candlesticks you gave her, and announced that she couldn't live without us, and that, from that moment on, she was the woman of our home."

A photograph fell out of the envelope: Myra in a man-sized apron with flour all over her arms, baking bread, and Annie, eleven years old, still skinny with freckles and pigtails, wearing a frilly pink dress and that crooked smile of hers. They didn't look like refugees at all.

I stared at little pink Annie standing next to her sister, and I remembered how they'd peed and cried in their sleep.

I was scared of my luck. No one in my family was killed, yet we'd survived the war scot-free, as the saying goes. How do the Scottish get to go unharmed? Is the anger of the war abated now that my dad is home? Or can it still come back and claim?

———∞◦◖◗◦∞———

Another spring has arrived. Today is a particularly bright, cold day, so beautiful it is hard to believe a world at war. I walk with Mom to the grocery shop. Food is still rationed, but we buy pretty brown speckled eggs. Mom tells me that eggs are a promise of new birth because they're round like the cycle of life.

"That's why people take them to houses of mourning."

"We must take them back to the store." Suddenly, I am riveted to the pavement. "We shouldn't have bought them. We're not a house of mourning!"

"Luv, our whole world is a house of mourning."

I picture the women of the world walking toward their homes carrying brown speckled eggs in their baskets. I see a universal binge on brown speckled eggs, people in the houses we pass celebrating the life cycle in rooms, rooms in which the windows are stripped of their blackness and stand open to the sights and sounds of peace; where mirrors are shrouded over like ghosts.

"I can't believe Sandra's father is gone," I'm scared to utter the real word for what happened to him.

"He's not gone. He's in our thoughts, isn't he? Thoughts that worry and hurt us...that has to count for something."

We pass the big pink house on the corner of Grant Street. It isn't pink anymore. Doesn't even seem big. It's a long time since the For Sale sign fell off. The plaster is flapping from its walls in sad paper-like folds, gray, laden with soot.

The children at school say the house is haunted. Of course, I don't believe them, but it is eerie and I make sure to avoid it when I'm on my own, just as I avoid the rows of bombed-out buildings in the center of town that gape like blind widows, black and toothless along the streets with rats running in and out of their skirts, just as I avoid looking at the crippled and maimed that now wait in bus lines and stop the traffic as they hobble across the road.

Mom goes inside. She walks around the garden. The windows are shattered, the garden overgrown with weeds and thorn bushes. Mom must have known the people who lived in that house before the war. When she comes out, she closes the gate as though preventing a dog or child from running into the street. With her handkerchief, she wipes the grime and the puddles of yesterday's rain from the top of the gate. Then she turns her back to it and hugs me.

"Their roses have died. But my little pinks are in bloom."

"What's that supposed to mean?"

"That we can go on living. May God forgive us."

"Oh, Mom! You're so dramatic."

She gives a half laugh. She squeezes my shoulder and we walk home with our arms around each other. She smells like a cinnamon bun, my mom does. A tear hangs in the corner of her eye, so I don't ask if what Miss Berliner said is true—that Hitler is alive and waiting.

CPSIA information can be obtained
at www.ICGtesting.com
Printed in the USA
BVHW041646190822
645018BV00015B/95